"Our first priority is getting you to safety."

Theo frowned. "Me? What do you mean? Why not the both of us?"

Whitney shrugged. "Look, this kind of life is what I signed up for. You didn't. In law enforcement, our primary objective is keeping civilians safe. The last thing I want is for you to get hurt because of me, especially after you've done so much to help me."

"Just because I'm not law enforcement doesn't mean I'm going to abandon you the first chance I get. If that were the case, we could have left the boat in that neighborhood in Plantation Key and gone our separate ways. I'm in this for the duration until both of us are safe."

Whitney looked into his sea-blue eyes and saw the truth behind his words. A warm feeling invaded her chest and seeped all the way down to her toes.

Kathleen Tailer is a senior attorney II who works for the Supreme Court of Florida in the office of the state courts administrator. She graduated from Florida State University College of Law after earning her BA from the University of New Mexico. She and her husband have eight children, five of whom they adopted from the state of Florida. She enjoys photography and playing drums on the worship team at Calvary Chapel in Thomasville, Georgia.

Books by Kathleen Tailer

Love Inspired Suspense

Under the Marshal's Protection
The Reluctant Witness
Perilous Refuge
Quest for Justice
Undercover Jeopardy
Perilous Pursuit
Deadly Cover-Up
Everglades Escape

Visit the Author Profile page at Harlequin.com.

EVERGLADES ESCAPE

KATHLEEN TAILER

LOVE INSPIRED SUSPENSE
INSPIRATIONAL ROMANCE

LOVE INSPIRED SUSPENSE
INSPIRATIONAL ROMANCE

Recycling programs
for this product may
not exist in your area.

ISBN-13: 978-1-335-40306-3

Everglades Escape

Love Inspired
22 Adelaide St. West, 40th Floor
Toronto, Ontario M5H 4E3, Canada
www.Harlequin.com

Printed in U.S.A.

And he said unto me, My grace is sufficient for thee:
for my strength is made perfect in weakness.
Most gladly therefore will I rather glory in my infirmities,
that the power of Christ may rest upon me.

Therefore I take pleasure in infirmities, in reproaches,
in necessities, in persecutions, in distresses
for Christ's sake: for when I am weak, then am I strong.
—2 Corinthians 12:9-10

For all of the employees of the Open Door Adoption Agency based in Thomasville, Georgia, who tirelessly work toward bringing home orphaned children from around the world. May God bless you!

Also, a special thank-you to Michael McElroy for lending me his technical expertise. Any mistakes herein are solely my own. Michael, you are truly amazing!

ONE

The first bullet hit the wood mere inches from Whitney Johnson's head and sent splinters all over her face and hair. The sound jolted her from her nap, and she sleepily shook the bits of wood away, still a bit confused by why she was hearing gunfire on a tour boat in the Atlantic Ocean. The second bullet hit her lounge chair, breaking one of the supports and making it lean to the left toward the deck of the vessel.

She didn't wait for a third bullet. Her law-enforcement training quickly kicked in and she ducked and rolled, immediately seeking refuge behind the wall that separated the captain's cabin from the main deck of the boat. The wall wasn't very thick, but it would at least offer some protection, and maybe serve as an adequate hiding place, as well. Screaming ensued from some of the other tourists, and more gunfire. Whitney desperately wished she had her firearm with her so she could defend herself, but she had purposefully left it at home before she'd boarded the plane for this vacation to Key West. She crouched as low to the deck as she could and pushed the door closed behind her.

The captain had allowed her to lie down in this secluded, quiet area of the boat when she had become nauseous, and there was no one else in sight. She doubted the shooters even knew she was there. In fact, she imagined the gunmen hadn't been aiming at her at all. Probably the random bullets were coming from high-powered rifles that had inadvertently found her resting place. Hopefully, that would be to her advantage.

She heard more yelling and it seemed like there were at least two different male voices ordering people around—maybe even three. It was muffled and hard to discern, but the angry tones made it clear that the tourists who had been expecting a relaxing day of watching dolphins and other sea life were now in serious trouble.

Whitney glanced through the slats of the door, once again wishing she had her gun with her. She was a US Marshal up in Tallahassee, and when on duty, she always had her weapon within reach. This time, however, she had left all vestiges of her normal life behind. She'd wanted a total break from her routine and had hoped this getaway was the answer. Whitney not only needed some R & R, but she also had a lot of thinking to do. Because only two days ago she'd gotten some devastating medical news that had shattered her hopes for the future.

The shouting seemed to be getting closer and

brought her back into the present. She pulled away from the door, but there wasn't really any place to hide in the small room. There was a narrow bunk, a desk, a dresser of sorts and a small bookshelf with books held in place by a braided leather strap. Thinking quickly, she locked the door, but realized the flimsy lock would do little to dissuade someone if they really wanted to get in. Her only option was to stay as quiet as possible and pray she went unnoticed until this nightmare was over.

"We've got the tourists cornered off and the men are depriving them of their valuables," a deep authoritarian male voice reported. "As far as they know, this is just an ordinary robbery."

Another man with a raspy tone answered. "This whole thing still makes me angry. If the captain hadn't tried to steal those drugs from us and sell them to our competitor, we wouldn't have had to board this boat in the first place. You and I would be frying steaks on the grill right now, enjoying the fruits of our labor. Now all of those witnesses will bring unwanted attention to our enterprise." Whitney heard clothing rustle and imagined the man was talking with his hands, accentuating his frustration.

"Well, he won't betray us again," the deep voice replied. "The captain is dead, but I made it look like part of the robbery. The rest of our mules will hear of it, and that's a good thing. Nobody else will try to steal drugs from us anytime soon, and that's a promise."

"You better be right." A floorboard creaked, as if the man was pacing on the deck. "Did you get the H?" A cold sweat traveled down Whitney's spine. "H" on the street stood for heroin. She surely hadn't expected to run into drug dealers on her vacation. Exactly what kind of boat was she on?

"Yeah, and it's already been transferred over to our boat. It was short by a third, though. The captain must have already delivered part of it to the other buyer, or else he got high with his friends. Who knows?"

"A *third*!" Raspy Voice bellowed. She heard a fist hit the wall and she jumped in surprise. "All of the China White and the pills?"

Whitney gritted her teeth. She knew China White was a powdered form of heroin often mixed with fentanyl, a *very* potent synthetic opioid. She also knew that heroin had recently been found in pressed pill form up the Eastern seaboard as far north as New Jersey. Some of the pills were a bluish-green and were pure heroin, while others looked just like pharmaceutical pills and contained a mixture of both heroin and fentanyl.

The heroin mix was new to Florida, and she'd just read a law-enforcement flyer on the drug last month when it had circulated through her office. Apparently, the source of the drug was a mystery that had remained unsolved—until now. It sounded like the men talking outside on the deck played a serious role in bringing the drug into the state. She edged closer to the door, the cop in her forcing her to try to discover the identity of the drug dealers she was hearing as they described their crimes.

"Yes, both the China White and the pills. I talked to Landry. He saw the captain forfeit his life and he knows that he's next if he can't deliver the missing batch. I gave him five days. Then we'll meet at Harper Key and he'll either deliver the missing product and add ten percent or meet his maker. The choice is up to him."

The man with the raspy voice spoke again. The man still didn't seem pleased, despite the additional information. "Okay. But can Landry take over the deliveries, or do we need to bring in somebody else? The captain has been doing this route for a while. I'm not sure I trust Landry."

"I've taken care of it, Lopez. Ronnie will stay with Landry for the next five days and keep an eye on the situation. Ronnie is a good man. He'll keep Landry in line." The deep voice became softer and Whitney had to strain to hear. "Does El Jefe know what's going on? The last time product disappeared, he killed everyone involved. I don't want to die because of that stupid captain and his greed."

Lopez's tone was hard and lethal when he answered. "Not yet, and we're going to keep it that way. Landry better come through with the missing batch, or we'll all pay the price."

Whitney moved one of the slats slightly so she could see better out of the door. The raspy-voiced man that apparently went by the name of Lopez was large and wearing a black T-shirt and jeans. He had a scar on his left cheek, about an inch long, that was a bit jagged, as if he hadn't been able to get medical care in time before the wound had started to heal. His hair was jet-black and short, and his skin was brown like leather yet mottled, as if he was a drinker. His eyes were dark and his nose was large, increasing his fearsome appearance. He was a big man, weighing well over two hundred pounds, and his arms were muscular and powerful, as if he worked out on a regular basis. There was no doubt in her mind that Lopez was a formidable adversary. He was also holding a hood in his hand. She guessed he had been wearing it earlier to hide his appearance.

Whitney wondered how many people knew the identity of the drug dealers bringing the White China into South Florida. She mentally kept a list. So far, there was Lopez; the guy with the deep voice he was talking to; and then two others named Landry and Ronnie who were somewhere else on the boat. Then there was the nameless "El Jefe," which meant "the chief" or "the boss" in Spanish.

She glanced over at the man with the deep voice. He was much shorter and had a smaller build than Lopez, but he also had a daunting presence. His hair and skin color matched his boss, but his eyes were a lighter brown and he was younger—almost half the bigger man's age. Both had pistols strapped to their hips, and Shorty had an AK-47 attached to his back.

Lopez suddenly moved toward the door that she was hiding behind and made another sweeping motion with his hand. "Did anyone check this room?"

Whitney took a sudden step back just as the big man rattled the doorknob and tested the lock. Had they seen her through the slats in the door? She hadn't thought it possible, but now she wasn't so sure. Her heart started thumping heavily in her chest and she tried hard to keep her breathing even and steady, even though she felt her adrenaline surge. Once again, she looked around the small room for anything that could be used as a weapon to defend herself. Her hopes sank as she found nothing.

"Ronnie said he swept the boat and had all the tourists up front," Shorty replied, a hint of worry in his tone.

Lopez suddenly lifted his leg and gave the door a vicious kick. It was a flimsy door and some of the wood hit Whitney as it exploded. She tried to get out of the way as pain shot through her knee and traveled up and down her right leg. She stepped back but was quickly grabbed by Lopez, who pulled her roughly out of the cabin.

"So who do we have here?" he murmured, his raspy voice filled with derision. Whitney said nothing. She was repulsed by the man's breath and the scent of cigar smoke emanating from his clothing.

"Looks like another tourist," the shorter man replied as he glanced at Whitney's bathing suit, cover-up shirt and shorts. "And a sunburned one at that."

"She's seen my face," Lopez said as he crudely pushed her toward the smaller guy. "And she heard us talking." The man caught her arms and held her tightly. Whitney didn't resist—at least not yet. She'd bide her time, wait for the chance to try to escape. She knew instinctively there might only be one opportunity, and she needed to wait for exactly the right moment.

"Kill her. Do it now."

The smaller man nodded and pulled her over to the edge of the boat as Lopez walked away from them, pulled the hood over his face and disappeared toward the front of the boat. Fear formed a ball in Whitney's abdomen, but she wasn't done yet. She hadn't come all the way to the Florida Keys to die at the hands of a drug dealer.

As her captor pulled out his pistol, he released her left arm. "Any last words?" he sneered. He raised the gun to her head, but she suddenly elbowed him hard in the stomach with her left arm then freed her right arm from his loosened grip and slammed his chin with an uppercut. The guy staggered back but still pulled the trigger. The gun fired harmlessly into the air. He tried to recover, but her unexpected onslaught had surprised him so much that his reactions were delayed. She took advantage of his shock and punched her assailant hard in the stomach, right where her elbow had hit, then struck his arm that was holding the gun. He lost his grip and the weapon clattered across the deck, landing a good fifteen feet away from them.

He made a grab for her, but she pulled back just in time and she brought both fists down hard on his back, forcing him to the deck in an ungainly sprawl. The guy moaned and didn't move, but Whitney knew he was not down for the count. There was only one way she could save herself. She turned and jumped into the ocean, hoping she had enough time to put some distance in between her and the boat before the criminals knew that she had escaped.

The water was a surprise to her system, but she recovered quickly and immediately started to swim in broad, solid strokes. She gave the deep-voiced man twenty seconds to pull himself together, grab the gun and return to the side of the boat, and she counted off the seconds in her head as she swam. Then she dove deeper into the water, praying that he hadn't seen which way she had gone. The three-foot swells that had previously made her nauseous were now her best friend and she said a second prayer, thanking God for the murky water and the waves that she hoped disguised her flight.

Whitney took a large breath and pushed herself deeper into the water, trying to stay under as long as possible. Her cover-up shirt and shorts were a navy blue, which she hoped also further camouflaged her. She knew her prayers were answered when she heard weapons firing to her right but not in her immediate vicinity. Whitney surfaced only long enough to take another breath and then continued swimming, trying to put even more distance between her and the boat.

Stopping to tread water, she scanned the area behind her, noting a speedboat tied on the port side of the tour boat. Surmising that the drug dealers had used the boat to approach and board the larger vessel, she hoped they wouldn't use it to chase her down. But anything was possible. At this point, she had to focus on escape. Turning, she didn't see any land in front of her, but kept swimming, knowing that several smaller islands made up the Florida Keys and there just had to be land out there somewhere.

Her heart lurched when she heard the speedboat zoom to life, and more gunfire, but thankfully none of it was close. Eventually, both boats were just dots on the horizon. She kept swimming, thankful for all of those diving and swimming classes she had taken to stay in shape back in college. An hour passed. Or was it two? She had no watch, and realized keeping track of the time would just deflate her hopes of survival.

So she kept swimming.

She swam until her arms started to feel like rubber and her chest hurt from the exertion. More time passed. She finally stopped to rest and tread water for a bit, desperately wishing she had a life preserver or other floatation device to use to keep her head above water. A small wave of panic swept over her, but she was determined to survive. Despite the medical news that had sent her to the Keys in the first place, she still had a long bucket list of things she wanted to accomplish in her life. She flipped over onto her back and just floated for a few minutes, resting a bit more from the exertion.

Dear God, please help me. The prayer was short but heartfelt. She had to find land soon if she was going to make it through this encounter. Her body was nearly spent.

Whitney turned and continued on, doing the best she could to stay alive. Last week she had been happy and carefree. Now it seemed like an eternity had passed. Between the news she had received at home and the events of this morning, her life had taken a distinct turn for the worse. She flipped onto her back again and took several deep breaths. The water was warm, so she wasn't worried about hypothermia, and since the waves made it hard to see, she used the sun to guide her. She was in good physical shape, but it was hard to keep her imagination from going wild as she remembered some of the scarier shark movies she had seen over the years. Did they even have great white sharks in this part of the world? She sure didn't want to find out.

She also knew she had to find land before her body gave out completely.

Theodore Roberts stepped over another wad of seaweed and continued his trek along the beach. He'd had a frustrating day, and his afternoon walk was proving to be less than satisfying since he'd been unable to solve the problem with his latest experiment in his medical lab. Why weren't the results what he'd hoped? He went over each step he'd taken again and again in his mind, but the solution didn't come. Kicking a large scallop shell in frustration, he watched it roll across the sand…and then land a few feet away from a woman's body.

The shock of seeing someone, especially an inert body on the sand being pushed by the waves, stunned him. Theo immediately ran to her side and gently pulled her from the water, separating her from a piece of driftwood and several palm tree fronds that she had evidently been using as a makeshift floatation device. He felt for a pulse and was instantly relieved when he found a beat. The woman moaned slightly as he repositioned her arm. He slowly pushed some of the hair out of her face and removed some debris that had snagged in her hair as he tried to get a better look at her.

She was beautiful.

Her blond hair was pulled back in a ponytail, but it was long enough that it had tangled around her face along with other strands that had come free during her time in the ocean. He brushed more of it away and appreciated her high cheekbones, full lips and porcelain skin, which was now quite red from sunburn. Guessing her age to be near thirty, he could see that she was fit and trim. He glanced at her right knee and noticed redness and swelling. Theo also noted she was shoeless and dirty, but she seemed otherwise unharmed.

He wondered how she had come to be on his beach, especially since this area was so secluded. Had she fallen off a cruise ship? Only wearing a simple bathing suit, shirt and shorts, she had no ID or jewelry to offer him any clues as to her identity. Still, her appearance screamed "tourist" and he imagined she was a dance instructor or in some other athletic profession when she wasn't vacationing in the Florida sun.

He quickly checked her for broken bones or other injuries. Finding none, he lifted her gingerly into his arms and headed toward his house.

A few minutes later, he had laid her carefully on his couch and was gently cleaning her face and arms with a cool washcloth. She had picked up quite a lot of sand and small bits of debris in her hair and clothing, so what she really needed was a shower. But even though she moaned from time to time, and coughed a bit, she was still coming in and out of consciousness. He assumed the cause was dehydration, but he couldn't get her to take a drink from the cup he offered and he had no straw or other way to get the water into her.

Theo gently untangled more of the debris that had snagged in her hair and then went to work on the tie that was holding her ponytail. Try as he might, though, he couldn't get it out of her hair. After a few minutes, he gave up and reached for a pair of scissors.

She awoke just after he snipped the tie and released her hair.

The next thing he knew she had chopped the scissors out of his hand, gripped his wrist and twisted his arm at such an awkward angle that sharp pain radiated up his arm and into his shoulder.

"Back off, buddy!" she snarled. "Or I'll break this arm and it will never work right again."

TWO

The scissors clattered as they landed on the floor across the room, but all Theo could think about was getting away from this woman's grip. He didn't want to hurt her or to get into a wrestling match, but he definitely wanted the pain to stop. He'd been wrong about her being a dance instructor. Now he was thinking she must be a female boxer or a karate sensei. She was much stronger than she looked.

"Whoa there, lady. Ease up. I'm only trying to help you."

She narrowed her eyes but didn't release him. Instead, she tightened her grip as she pulled herself up to a sitting position. Theo imagined she felt less vulnerable that way, but at this point, he didn't really care. The pain was getting worse, and he was done being nice. He tried to wrench his arm free, but when he attempted to pull away, he found her grip unbreakable.

Her eyes darted around the room and he could

see the distrust and wariness in those gray depths.
"Who are you? Where am I?"

He grimaced. "I'm happy to answer your questions—after you release my wrist."

She met his eyes. "How do I know I can trust you?" A raised eyebrow accompanied her question, yet despite the fierceness in her countenance, he still felt a sizzle of attraction. It irritated him beyond measure. He did *not* want to feel any sort of attraction to this woman who was seconds away from breaking his arm.

He gritted his teeth and took a deep breath. When he spoke, he tried to keep his voice as low and nonthreatening as possible. "You don't. But I'm the one that just pulled you out of the water and brought you in here. If I weren't trying to help you, I would have left you out on the beach." He relaxed his stance but still pulled against her grip. "Please? I promise, I'm not going to hurt you."

"Who are you?" she asked again with suspicious eyes.

"My wrist?" He raised his own eyebrow.

She relented and released his arm. In the same movement she skittered backward out of his reach, nearer the far end of the couch.

He rubbed his shoulder wistfully. This woman was fiercer and tougher than any female he ever remembered meeting. He took a step back, giving her the space she was seeking. "Theo Roberts, at your service. And you are?"

She ignored his question, obviously still distrusting him, then slowly scanned the room again. "Where am I?"

He shrugged and sat in a chair a few feet away, hoping his docile appearance would help put her at ease. She was obviously not a tourist that had fallen off of a cruise ship as he had originally suspected. There was more to the story here.

Much more.

"You're in my home. I'm an aquatic biogeochemist, and I live on this island by myself. I'm studying bleaching and wound healing in staghorn coral so we can restore the coral reefs. It's a pretty small island, and gives me the privacy I need to work." He pushed his rimless glasses farther up on his nose in a slow, deliberate motion. "You washed up on my beach about an hour ago—at least, that's when I found you. I was trying to get the seaweed and other things out of your hair when you woke up. I had to cut the hair tie out because it was so tangled."

She subconsciously reached behind her head and felt her loosened hair, then noticed the wad of seaweed with a few of her hairs still attached sitting in a heap on the floor.

The motion accented her arms and Theo felt his heart beat against his chest as he appreciated her well-toned muscles. The feelings surprised him and he was taken aback at his own reaction. He hadn't even looked at another woman or felt an attraction to anyone since his wife and daughter had perished in a car accident almost four years ago. The fact that he was noticing this woman now filled him with self-loathing. There was a reason why he was living off the grid, completely isolated from most of society. He didn't seek or want the company.

He turned his head away, suddenly very interested in the fringe on his chair pillow. "You're a bit dehydrated, which is why you probably feel dizzy and faint. Can you drink that?" He turned his head toward the cup sitting on an end table then swiveled back. He couldn't very well talk to the pillow.

She narrowed her eyes again, but eventually picked it up and warily looked inside. "What is it?"

"It's just water. Bottled water, actually. There's no fresh water on the island that's fit to drink, but I get supplies delivered once a month. Drink up. I have plenty."

She took a sip and, apparently satisfied, tipped the cup and finished it off quickly. He stood and the motion made her instantly put up her arms in a defensive motion.

"Easy. I just want to pour you some more water."

She let him get close enough to refill her cup from a bottle sitting on the coffee table, and watched him carefully as he sat back down again. "What time is it?"

Theo glanced at his watch. "About 7:00 p.m. It's Thursday." He surveyed her face, looking for clues about his guest. "Who are you? How did you end up in the water?"

She finished off her drink again and put the glass by the bottle on the coffee table.

To his relief, she seemed to relax somewhat and it appeared that she'd made a decision to trust him, at least a little. "My name is Whitney. Whitney Johnson. I was on a marine wildlife tour when a boatload of drug dealers came aboard. Apparently, the captain had a side business working as a mule, and he got greedy and wanted to sell some of the product to a different buyer. The drug dealers objected."

She reacted to a sound he made with a derisive smile. "Yeah, I know. Big surprise. Anyway, I saw one of the leaders and heard him giving orders to one of his men. He must be someone important. He'd been wearing a hood earlier to disguise himself but didn't realize I was there when he took it off. When they discovered I had seen and heard them, they decided to kill me. So I jumped into the ocean, and started swimming to avoid being shot. I was in the water for quite a while. I don't remember much after that."

Theo quirked a brow. "You're lucky to be alive. Where did you sail from?"

"We left Key West around nine this morning. The seas were a little bit rough and I started feeling sick, so I went to lie down near the captain's quarters. That's why I wasn't with the others—having sea sickness saved me." She released a breath. "I don't know what ultimately happened to everybody else on the boat. I know they shot the captain but, hopefully, the others got safely back to the dock."

Theo took a sip from his own cup. "Then you got lucky twice. Usually the water around here is so clear that a swimmer would definitely stand out and make an easy target, but the storm we had last night and the rough water churned up the sand and reduced the visibility."

Whitney shook her head. "It wasn't luck. It was God. He was protecting me. I started praying the second I heard the first shot."

Theo shrugged, unwilling to argue with her. He believed in God, but still had the taste of bitterness in his mouth from the death of his wife and child. Their deaths had been shocking and abrupt. He wasn't sure why God had allowed them to die, and the guilt and anger he still felt ate him up inside. In any case, after living through that experience, he wasn't about to give God credit for saving the woman in front of him. He decided to change the subject.

"You'll probably want a shower. I live off solar power and lead a very simple life, so I imagine it's not what you're used to, but it will have to do."

"A shower would be great, but I'm actually pretty hungry. Do you have anything to eat?"

He stood, motioned for her to follow him, then walked across the room to where a small table and two chairs sat near the compact kitchen.

Whitney stood but didn't follow him. When he

turned, he noticed a look of wariness in her eyes. "Did you say you lived here alone?" she asked.

Theo shrugged, hoping his motions were still non-threatening to his guest. He wanted to put her at ease if he could. Pulling out a pineapple from a basket sitting on the kitchen counter, he began slicing off the peel. It was odd having someone in his house. He had been alone on this island for almost two years, and rarely had human company beyond the man who delivered his supplies on a monthly basis. And the guy never came into his home.

"Yes, I live by myself. This island isn't a named key, and only measures about forty acres from one end to the other. Very few people even know it exists, and I never have visitors."

Whitney finally crossed the room and took a seat at the table. "What do you do here? I mean, I heard you say you were a scientist, but how do you accomplish what you need to do when you are so isolated?"

Theo finished peeling the fruit, sliced it and put it on a plate in front of his guest. "I work on a lot of experiments mostly. I have a small lab in a room over there." He motioned to the left. "I collect the data and send in my findings once a month."

She absorbed that information but didn't comment, then forked a piece of the pineapple he'd offered. "I need to call the police—" She took a bite of the fruit and her face lit up at the taste. She quickly ate several more pieces and swallowed them hungrily. "Wow, that is amazing." After wiping her mouth with the napkin he'd provided, she went back to her original thought. "I have to report what happened as soon as possible and make sure those people are safe."

Theo grimaced. "That's going to be kind of difficult."

Whitney straightened, instantly on alert. "And why is that?" she asked, her voice taking on an edge of steel.

"Because I don't have a phone."

Whitney was incredulous. Who in this day and age didn't have a phone and access to the internet? She wasn't from a big city, but still, she didn't know a single person between the age of fifteen and seventy that didn't own a phone, and 90 percent of those had smartphones with constant access to the internet. In fact, she was the best researcher on her team of US Marshals, and a large part of her work was searching for information on the net on a regular basis. At this point, she couldn't even imagine trying to do her job, or even going through life itself, without it.

Had she just landed on *Gilligan's Island*? She almost expected the Skipper or the Professor to come walking up. She glanced over at her host. Theo didn't look anything like the professor from the old sitcom. Instead, the man before her was lean and strong, with tanned skin and amazing blue eyes that seemed to see right through her. His hair was short and chestnut brown with reddish highlights brought out by the sun. She saw a bit of curl, and imagined he kept it short to keep those curls under control.

He wore rimless glasses that made him look the part of a scientist like he claimed to be, but he'd also donned a simple white T-shirt and khaki shorts, as if he was on vacation. What kind of scientist abandoned society and the internet, both of which had so much to offer, to study dying coral reefs on a desolate island?

Whitney was a people person. She would go stark raving mad if she didn't have someone to talk to on a regular basis. How did this guy do it?

She glanced around at her surroundings again. The house was simple and, to her surprise, now that she was really looking at it, she noticed it was round instead of square or rectangular like most homes. The inside was basically one large room that included both a living room, a kitchen area and an office of sorts. A large wooden desk, covered in books and papers, stood testimony to his work. A couple of doors led off from the main room, and she imagined they led to a bedroom or two and a bathroom. The windows had no curtains, and she could tell that the house itself was on stilts and stood a good ten feet off the ground. Tropical foliage made it hard to see more than a few feet in any direction.

She turned back to Theo. The place was great—for a vacation. She still couldn't wrap her head around the fact that he lived here on a year-round basis. She had to be missing something. What was the allure?

"Okay, so no phone. How do you communicate with the outside world?"

Theo shrugged. "I don't."

Her eyes rounded. "What about the internet?"

"I don't use it."

"How do you do any sort of scientific research without the internet?" She knew her tone was incredulous, but she just couldn't help it.

He smiled, and it did something funny to her insides. She pushed the feelings away. "You've heard of books, right?" he asked.

She scoffed, but arguing about the benefits of using up-to-date information on the internet for research was way down on her priority list. "What about a boat?"

"Does a kayak count?"

She grimaced. "Okay, so what do you do for supplies?"

"I have a man that makes deliveries once a month."

"How do you contact him when you need supplies?" she asked.

"I don't. I just make a list each month. When he makes a delivery, I give him the list of what I need for him to bring during his next trip, as well as my notes and latest research that he sends on to my team. He comes on or near the first day of each month like clockwork."

Whitney had visions of the many times she had gotten in after working a midnight shift, had no food in the house, and had to run out to the twenty-four-hour grocery store around the corner—not to mention the number of doughnut runs she had made at odd hours when the craving hit her. She couldn't imagine limiting herself to shopping for supplies a month at a time, or the planning it would take to do so. Mr. Theodore Roberts was an odd man, to say the least.

Still, he was attractive in an intriguing sort of way.

Even though it was evening, it was still pretty hot outside. There was no air-conditioning, and the ceiling fan did little to alleviate the heat. As a result, Theo's skin shone with a thin layer of perspiration that accentuated his muscles as he moved. His hands caught her attention as he reached for a piece of pineapple and took a bite. She watched avidly as he reached for another. His fingers were long and powerful, and his motions were deliberate and exact. She also couldn't help but note that his nails were straight and clean, and his skin was smooth, stretched tightly over the sinew and bone that moved easily as he ate.

Whitney stopped her woolgathering and returned to the present. Her vacation was over. She had to report this crime and let local law enforcement know what she had learned before the evidence was destroyed and the culprits escaped. "So, what do you do if you have an emergency?"

Theo shrugged again and finished off the last of the fruit. "I don't have emergencies. My life is pretty routine."

"Do you have a gun, or any other way to protect yourself?"

He shook his head. "I've never had a need before. Like I said, nobody ever comes by."

Whitney blew out an exasperated breath. Maybe his life had been simple and mundane, but she had an uneasy feeling that all of that was about to change. Those drug dealers meant business, and she was afraid that it was only a matter of time before they showed up knocking at Theo's door. She had seen Lopez's face, and heard details about their operation. These criminals wouldn't just assume she was dead. They would need proof. This calm, innocent man in front of her had suddenly been thrust into more danger than he could possibly have imagined.

THREE

Whitney had been too exhausted to do more talking, so Theo had showed her to his guest bedroom where she had promptly fallen asleep within seconds of her head hitting the pillow. The next morning, he was up early at the usual time and sat at the small kitchen table, a cup of coffee in one hand and a muffin in the other, waiting for her to wake up and see what the day would bring.

She finally emerged and he found himself ready for the company, which was a strange feeling for him after living such a solitary existence for such a long time. He had also never met anyone like Whitney Johnson before in his entire life. He still had a lot of unanswered questions about her floating around in his mind, but one thing he was sure of—she was the most vivacious person he had ever come across. Her attitude and energy were not just intriguing, they were *infectious*.

Once she was in the living room, he motioned to the other chair at the table.

"Good morning," he intoned. "I hope I didn't wake you."

"Good morning back," she replied, her voice still raspy from sleep. She shook her head and brushed some of the hair out of her eyes, then started toward him.

"Coffee?"

When she nodded, he poured her a cup. "I hope you like bran muffins." She sat and he pushed a plate of muffins and fruit, then a mug, in her direction. "Sorry. I don't have cream or sugar, but I do have some honey if you want it."

"No thanks. I take my coffee black." She grabbed a muffin and took a bite then regarded him thoughtfully. "Hey, this is pretty good."

He took a sip of his coffee. "Thanks. It's not much, but I throw a batch together every now and then. I usually add some sort of fruit, if I can. These have cranberries in them." He raised an eyebrow. "How are you feeling?"

Whitney swallowed. "I'm a bit stiff from all of that swimming, and my skin is on fire because of the sunburn. I'm happy to be alive, though, and I could sure use a shower this morning, if it's okay."

"Sure thing," Theo replied. He had offered her a shower a second time last night, but she had been so exhausted from her ocean swim that she'd settled for rinsing off with a washcloth and going straight to bed. "I think I have some aloe around here, too. That will help with the sunburn after the shower."

She finished off her muffin, as well as several more pieces of pineapple, then brushed the muffin crumbs into her hand and dumped them into the wastebasket. She was back a moment later. "So, if I remember correctly, today is only the seventeenth. If your supplier doesn't come until the end of the month, I'm afraid you might be stuck with me for a while, unless you can think of a way for me to get off this island that we haven't already discussed."

Theo took a sip of his coffee and regarded her thoughtfully. "Yes, I've considered that. Unless you want to try to kayak to Key West, I think you're going to be here for a couple of weeks."

She looked into his eyes, seeking, and he hoped he was doing an adequate job of masking his frustration. A visitor for a day or two, he could handle. He even found the thought somewhat fascinating since Whitney was such an enigma and so different from his own calm, studious personality.

As intriguing as he found her, however, her presence did make him somewhat uncomfortable, and the prospect of being with her for a couple of weeks made him downright anxious. She was a lively, beautiful young woman, whereas he was a boring, self-isolated introvert. He didn't have the slightest idea how to entertain her. Still, he was trying desperately to be polite. It wasn't her fault she was there. He needed to remember that.

As if she could read his mind, she touched his hand lightly, then withdrew. "I'm really sorry I've invaded your privacy and inconvenienced you. I'll do my best to stay out of your way until the end of the month."

He swallowed. "I appreciate that. I have plenty of food and water and some clothes you can borrow. We'll make it work until the supplier comes."

"Well, in the meantime, those drug dealers could show up at any minute. We need to do something to prepare for their arrival."

He set down his mug. Having even more visitors was not something he had contemplated. "Really? Why?"

"They haven't found my body, so until they do, I'm a loose end. They seemed like a pretty professional organization. My survival was a mistake, and they'll want to remedy that fact as soon as possible. They're probably searching for me as we speak, and I'd guess they won't give up until they finish the job."

Theo really didn't like the idea of criminals running around on his island. "Well, what would you suggest we do to prepare? I already told you, I don't have a gun, a phone or a boat." He'd never needed to defend himself in the past, but now he was starting to think about it on a regular basis.

"Do you have any sort of surveillance system?"

His brow furrowed at her question and she laughed at his expression. "No, I suppose not."

Theo stood and motioned for her to follow him. "I'll have to think about all of this. In the meantime, let's get you a shower and take care of your sunburn.

I'll get something rigged up for you, and then I promise to stay on the other side of the house to give you some privacy."

She followed him outside and down the stairs to ground level. At first, he worried a bit about her wounded knee and managing the stairs, but she seemed to do okay, and he decided to address it with her after she'd had a chance to clean up. He pointed to a smaller building, also on stilts, and connected by decking. "Well, you've seen the house, such that it is. That smaller building over there is my lab. There aren't any other structures on the island besides a dock down at the south end." Then he motioned to the space under the two buildings. "I have some fishing and diving equipment down here, as well as the aforementioned kayak, and some exercise machines. Feel free to sort through them if you want to see if there is anything there you can use while you're here to pass the time." He directed her to a small shower area that was rigged against the pilings. "Here we go."

Theo could see her surprise, but was pleased that she took it in stride. This woman definitely seemed out of her element, but she was doing her best to be as flexible as possible. He appreciated her efforts. He also acknowledged that there wasn't much to the accommodations he was offering—just some wooden slats to stand on, and a pipe running up the wall to a rusted silver showerhead. A lever with a short rope attached to the pipe completed the setup.

Strangely, he almost wished he had more to offer. "I have limited water, and it isn't heated," he told her apologetically. "You'll have to rinse, turn the water off while you wash, and then rinse again." He raised his hands. "And don't worry. I'll rig up something to give you some privacy. Like I said before, I'm the only one living on this island, so I never worried about an enclosure, but I'll be sure not to bother you. You'll have this all to yourself."

He opened a medium-size bin next to the shower area and pulled out a towel and a faded navy T-shirt. Then he opened a second box and pulled out a pair of slip-on soft rubber clogs. "You can use these while you rinse out your clothes. There is also shampoo and soap you can use."

He reached back into the bin and withdrew a clothesline and a tarp. In a few short minutes, he had rigged up a shower stall that he hoped would give his guest some measure of comfort. He threaded the line through the loops in the tarp and secured it to a bolt attached to his stairway. "There you go. Enjoy your shower."

She watched him go back up the stairs, then limped over and stepped into the makeshift shower. Giving the rope on the lever a trial tug, she watched as water started to gurgle out of the showerhead. Okay, maybe this was going to work, after all. The water was cool, but it was already so hot outside that it felt refreshing, especially with her sunburn.

Whitney's shower was quick since she wanted to be as mindful as she could of the limited water supply Theo had mentioned. She could tell that her presence was bothering him, and she didn't want to outstay her welcome or to use up all of his supplies during her first few hours on the island. His words had been friendly enough, but she was an expert on reading people. Theo was like a closed book tucked away high on a bookshelf where no one could touch or open it. He wanted to be by himself, and while he was making an amazing effort to make her feel welcome, she was sure he would rejoice as soon as she was gone. Hopefully, she could get a ride off of this island as soon as his supplier showed up with his monthly deliveries.

It bothered her that the delay would possibly hinder the investigation into the crimes that had occurred on the tour boat, but she hoped that law enforcement had already become involved in the murder and robbery. She said a quick prayer, asking God to be with the victims and to help the police make the appropriate arrests. Drug rings operating in Florida were all too common, and this one was particularly dangerous due to the heroin and fentanyl they were bringing into the state.

Having finished her shower, she felt amazingly refreshed, even though her newly cleaned bathing suit and shorts were still a bit damp. She was immensely thankful for Theo's dry T-shirt which was a welcome addition to her wardrobe. It was too big for her, but it felt good to be wearing at least one piece of clothing that wasn't wet, especially after her long stint in the ocean. It felt so good to be clean! For a while there, she'd thought she was going to end up like a giant salty prune.

Suddenly she heard a faint noise outside of the shower. A jolt of adrenaline swept up her spine and she froze, listening carefully. A moment passed. Then another. It might have only been a bird roosting nearby, but in her current circumstances, it paid to be careful. She waited another second or two, and then, hearing nothing further, she screwed the cap back on the shampoo and put it back on the shelf.

She stepped out of the shower enclosure and found herself staring right into the barrel of a 9mm handgun.

"That's far enough, lady."

Whitney raised her hands in a motion of surrender and whimpered to make the gunman think she was weak and powerless. The man was taller than she was, outweighing her by a good seventy pounds. He had an evil smile on his face, as if he enjoyed his work a little too much. He was also young and overconfident. He clearly didn't see her as a threat, which was exactly what she wanted.

"Move slowly, lady. Step over here." He motioned with the gun he held in his right hand toward the stairway leading to the house and then whistled. "Lopez is going to be so happy that I found you. He's got people looking everywhere."

Whitney raised an eyebrow. "Lopez? Who's that?" She limped to where he motioned, making exaggerated movements, as if she was in a great deal of pain. Then she swiveled back around to face him. Suddenly she grabbed the gun barrel with her left hand and moved her head and torso out of the line of fire. Then her right hand instantly shot out and chopped the man's wrist, loosening his grip and forcing the gun back around to face her aggressor.

She'd acted based upon all of her law-enforcement training and experience, knowing that the element of surprise would only work in her favor for a few seconds at best. Because of her actions, he had no choice but to suffer a broken wrist or release the gun. She took it from him, just as her left hand fisted and caught him in the throat. The entire set of motions took about three seconds.

He gurgled in shock and fell back a step as she verified that the safety was off and the weapon was ready to fire if needed. The man's eyes widened when he realized his gun was now in his victim's hands and pointed directly at his head. Any amusement he had showed before had now turned to anger. But he was helpless to do anything but glare at the woman before him.

"On the ground now!" she ordered.

He shook his head. "You don't know who you're dealing with. You'll be dead within twenty-four hours." His tone was hoarse as he tried to breathe despite the blow to his neck, but he was putting as much bravado as he could into the threat.

"Not likely. Get down on the ground." Her voice was firm and left no room for argument. Still, she could see in the man's eyes that he was considering making a grab for the weapon.

"Try it and I'll put a bullet between your eyes," she stated in a matter-of-fact tone. "In case you're wondering—I'm an expert shot."

He must have believed her because he nodded slightly then slowly got down on his knees and intertwined his fingers behind his head. His embarrassment and loathing were palpable.

"All the way down. On your stomach. Now."

The assailant grimaced but did as he was told. She kept the gun trained on him with one hand, but used the other hand to pull at the knot in the clothesline that Theo had used to make her shower enclosure. She didn't have any handcuffs with her, so she didn't have much choice but to tie the man up with whatever she could find. Thankfully, she knew quite a bit about tying knots in such a way that the guy would not be escaping anytime soon.

She used one end of the cord to tie his hands together and secure them to the bottom of the handrail of the stairs. The other end, she used to secure his feet and then tied them to the nearby trunk of a small palm tree. He was still facedown on the ground, stretched firmly between the bindings, which made it impossible for him to do more than roll a few inches in either direction.

Once she was finished, Whitney turned her attention to the house. "Theo?" she called. There was no answer. She tried again. "Theo?"

There was still no answer and a sense of dread swept over her. Had they killed the handsome scientist who had pulled her from the ocean?

FOUR

Whitney quickly inspected the drug dealer's trusses one last time, then immediately started up the steps to the house, still armed with the guy's weapon. It was slow going with her injured knee, but she moved as rapidly as possible, her heart pounding with the fear of what she might find.

She owed a lot to Theo Roberts, and she didn't think she was overstating it by saying that he had saved her life. She had gotten dehydrated during her swim, and might have died as a result if he hadn't found her on the beach and taken care of her. Now, to thank him, she had brought drug dealers to his door, and for all she knew, he was bleeding out from a bullet wound while she had been washing her hair. A wave of crushing guilt swept over her, and she said a quick prayer for Theo's safety.

Searching swiftly, she found him in the room where she had slept, lying on the floor. She stowed the gun in her waistband and rushed to his side. "Theo! Are you okay?"

He moaned at her voice and rubbed his head. He had apparently been knocked out, and was just now coming out of it. She helped him to a sitting position and gently examined his head. There was a large bump on the back of his skull, but thankfully no blood.

"I will be. Somebody hit me. I've got quite a headache." He quickly met her eyes. "Are you okay?"

"I'm fine. Did you see who did it?"

"No. I was putting some things away, and the next thing I know, I'm waking up with a knot on my head."

"Well, I caught a guy by the shower and have him tied up outside. He's one of the drug dealers. Hopefully, he's the only one on the island, but I can't be sure. I didn't recognize him, but he mentioned that Lopez was looking for me, which is the name of the leader I met on the boat." She glanced around the sparsely furnished room. "Can I help you to a chair? I want to search the perimeter and make sure he doesn't have a friend out there somewhere, but I don't want to leave you on the floor."

"Sure." He stretched out his hand. She took it and pulled him to a standing position, but he didn't take a seat after, as she'd expected. "I'm okay. Really. I'll help you search. I know your knee is hurting."

"Probably not any worse than your head." Instead of rubbing her leg, she rubbed her arm absently, her hand still tingling from the contact with the dashing marine scientist. In fact, at the moment, she barely noticed her knee. The feelings surprised her. Why was she so affected by Theo Roberts? But right now she didn't have time to think about this strange attraction that was suddenly popping up at the worst possible moment. She needed to be engrossed in ensuring their safety.

Whitney pushed the uncomfortable thoughts aside and focused on the issue at hand. Was there another perp, or had the guy she had tied up outside come alone? And how had someone from Lopez's organization found her so quickly? She imagined they had several people out searching, but she was truly surprised at the speed of their success.

Regardless, she needed to contact law enforcement immediately. But there was no way to do so with Theo's current setup. However, the drug dealer's presence wasn't all bad news. Maybe the perp could actually help her get off this island. She'd frisked him when she'd tied him up and hadn't found a phone. Yet he must have arrived by boat, so maybe he had left it behind when he had made his way to the house. With or without a phone, having a boat at her disposal was indeed a gift from God. Whitney had never driven one before, but how hard could it be?

She would just have to be a quick study because she would do whatever it took to get back to civilization.

Search the perimeter. Theo shook his head as her words replayed in his mind. He sure hadn't guessed her occupation correctly. She had to be military—or law enforcement. No one else would use a phrase like that. Even so, he still felt protectiveness surge within him. It even overwhelmed the frustration he was feeling ever since she had invaded his sanctuary.

And now it wasn't just Whitney that had violated his privacy. At least one drug dealer was also on his island. That probably meant more would soon be on the way. He had the sinking feeling that his life had just drastically changed in more ways than he could even imagine. The thought made him break out in a cold sweat. He was a man of consistency and schedule. Living an orderly life was of the upmost importance to him. He didn't like spontaneity. Or change. But he couldn't leave Whitney to face this threat on her own, even if he barely knew her and even if she was the most capable female he had ever met. Good grief—she had already disarmed one drug dealer. He'd seen her pull a gun from her waistband right before she'd left the room and, since he didn't own one and she hadn't arrived with one, there was only one other explanation. Absently rubbing the bump on his head, he followed her into the living room, keeping an eye out for anything that seemed out of place or would hint that there were more criminals lurking around the corner.

They found nobody else in the house, or on the property surrounding the small structures. After doing a thorough search, they ended up back by the shower. Theo was shocked to see the size of the man

Whitney had bested, and made a mental note never to make her angry. The guy was at least twice her size. Whitney Johnson was one tough cookie.

"So when are your friends coming?" she asked the modern-day pirate who was still trussed on the ground like a Thanksgiving turkey.

He ignored her and purposefully looked away.

She shrugged. "It doesn't matter. We'll be ready." Theo found her air of confidence a bit unnerving. How could they possibly be ready when they had only one gun between them, no additional ammunition and no way to call for help?

"Theo, do you have those other surprises ready for when his friends arrive?" She winked at him out of the drug dealer's line of vision, so he followed her lead, not sure what to expect but trusting her to know what she was doing.

"Yes. Everything is good to go." He instilled as much enthusiasm in his voice as he could, realizing she was speaking for the drug dealer's ears rather than his own. As far as he knew, the only surprises waiting for anyone were the pineapple and mangos he had decided to cut up for the rest of their breakfast that were still in a glass bowl on the dining room table. His stomach rumbled at the thought. He hadn't had much to eat with his coffee, and he imagined Whitney was still famished after her day in the ocean—one muffin and some fruit wouldn't be enough to sustain her. Still, with all of the adrenaline they were both feeling, it was hard to think too seriously about food right now.

Theo wasn't a military or law-enforcement officer, but he knew enough to figure that their next move had to be going to the dock where he usually met the man who brought his supplies. That was really the only place a boat could land on the island, and they had to learn more about this criminal who had assaulted them and be as prepared as possible for when others arrived, if they weren't there already. He didn't own anything but a kayak himself, but this attacker must have left some sort of vessel at the dock. Perhaps he had also left something useful in the boat that would help them neutralize this threat.

Theo didn't want to leave the island. His lab was here. His *life* was here. Sure, he lived a simple existence, but he was happy. Or if not happy, he was at least satisfied. And in the space of only twenty-four hours, he had suddenly lost everything familiar. Yet he couldn't ignore the fact that more criminals were bound to show up sooner or later looking for his new guest, and they would probably think nothing of killing Whitney and him if they got in their way.

He caught Whitney's eye. "If you can watch him for a minute or two, I'll go grab us a few things from inside the house." If nothing else, Theo was a planner. He tried to prepare for every contingency. Even though he didn't want to leave, he knew being forced to leave was a distinct possibility. He also didn't want to have the lady going up and down the stairs any more than necessary with her injured knee. But he realized they might need some supplies if they found themselves in a precarious situation at the waterfront or if they couldn't return.

Whitney nodded at him. "Sure thing. My friend here and I will get to know each other a little better while you're gone."

Theo took the stairs two at a time and grabbed a backpack as he passed into the small living area. He didn't want to take much with him. After all, they might be coming back to the house after they checked the dock. Still, he had the sinking feeling that he wouldn't be returning to this house anytime soon.

He started in the bathroom. Taking up a small bottle of pain reliever, two Ace bandages, some tape, a bottle of aloe and some toilet paper, he threw them into the bag. Then he returned to the kitchen, filled two water bottles and added those along with several power bars, some beef jerky and the rest of the bran muffins he had made that morning that were now in a plastic bag. He took one more look around, grabbed another bag and poured the cut fruit into it before sealing it and throwing it into the backpack, as well.

He found Whitney pretty much the same as when he had left her. "Did you get anywhere?"

"No." She shrugged. "Suddenly he has forgotten how to speak English."

Theo smiled. "Isn't that a shame?" He motioned at a worn wooden chair leaning against a tree a short distance away and out of earshot of their captive. "Care to have a seat?"

She raised an eyebrow. "Why?"

He pulled out one of the Ace bandages and the tape. "I'm going to fix up your knee a bit."

"Are you a doctor?"

He paused as a twinge of pain hit his chest, but finally, he answered her question. "Yes, I am. Well, actually, I used to be." He could see the surprise in her eyes, but she did as he'd asked. He checked her knee and wrapped it, then adjusted the tightness of the bandage to make sure it wouldn't affect her circulation. Then he helped her back to her feet.

"How does that feel?"

She smiled gratefully. "Better. Thanks so much." There was a strange look in her eyes, but he ignored it, not sure how to decipher it anyway. He had been much better at reading people before his last two years of self-imposed isolation. He reached over to a plant that was growing under the tree and broke off two of the leaves. "Here. This is aloe vera. It will help with your sunburn. I've got some more in the backpack, but this will be a good start." He broke one stalk in two, squeezed out the sticky juice and then gently applied it to her cheeks, nose and forehead. His fingers marveled at the softness of her skin, and lingered a moment before he pulled away.

"Does that feel better?" Suddenly his mouth was dry and he was having trouble talking. Did he sound as much like an idiot as he felt?

He was relieved when she broke eye contact and popped the other piece of aloe open and started applying it to her shoulders and neck. "Yes, thank you. It's making a huge difference the second it touches my skin. I recognized the ginger plants and bird-of-paradise you have growing around here, but I had no idea what aloe looked like before it gets bottled and sold at the grocery store."

"It's an amazing plant," he murmured, glad the awkward moment had passed. He motioned with his hand toward a well-worn path off to the left that led into the vegetation. "Follow me?"

"Sure thing," she agreed.

Theo slung the backpack over his shoulder and started down the path, trying not to move too hurriedly for fear of making her knee injury even worse. When they were almost to the dock, he suddenly heard voices coming right toward them. He quickly pulled her off the path and angled them low behind a stand of palmetto, hoping they were concealed.

"We have company," he whispered. "They're almost right on top of us."

FIVE

"She'll run to Baker. They always do. And once she does, we'll have her." The drug dealer's tone was emphatic as the two passed only a few feet from Whitney and Theo's hiding place. His voice was rough and deep, as well as heavily accented.

"Lopez doesn't want it to take that long," the other dealer replied. "He wants this problem to go away now. Today, if possible." This man's voice was more nasally and higher-pitched. "She couldn't have swum this far anyway. She was just a tourist. She's probably already fish food at the bottom of the ocean."

The first man laughed. "You tell Lopez that. He wants proof. If you think a fish got her, he'll want you to go catch the fish that ate her and bring it to him on a platter."

"I wouldn't mind spending a day like that, reeling in a marlin or two—"

"Stay focused!" the deep voice ordered. "Jose was supposed to call in and we still haven't heard from him. We don't know what we're gonna find here."

"Jose is a fool," the nasally voiced dude replied. "There's probably not even service out here, but even if there is, the guy is an idiot. Three times, he's let the battery die on his phone. He's all brawn and no brains. This island isn't that big, so I'm sure we'll find him sleeping under a tree or something. Apparently, there's only one building on the entire island. He should have reported in already…"

Their voices faded as they continued on the path toward the house. Whitney let a few moments pass then quickly stood. "We don't have much time. We need to get to that dock and find Jose's boat before they find him tied up on the ground." She followed Theo back to the path that led to the dock. "Who's Baker?" she asked quietly as they hurried along.

"I was hoping you knew," Theo answered, also in a low tone. "I don't know anyone named Baker."

It didn't take the two very long to reach the dock. The wooden planking extended about thirty feet into the water and ended with a floating rectangle of wood about eight feet wide that was designed to rise and drop with the prevailing tides. Large metal loops secured around heavy wooden posts the diameter of telephone poles kept the dock itself in place.

They saw two boats tied to the horn cleats. There was a 21-foot center-console boat on one side of the floating dock and a smaller 18-foot walk-through vessel on the other. They waited cautiously, still partly concealed by the foliage, until they could ascertain that no one was guarding either boat.

Finally, Whitney motioned that it was safe to leave their hiding places. "Looks like we're alone. Why don't you search the larger boat and I'll check out the smaller one."

"Deal," Theo answered. "Anything special we're looking for?"

"Keys to ride away in one of these boats would be nice," she said with a smile. "But some sort of phone or other way to call for help would be a great find, too, if there is one available. I'm not picky at this point." She raised an eyebrow. "Do you know how to shoot a gun?"

Theo shrugged. "I've done some target shooting, but that's about it, and it was a long time ago." He motioned with his hand. "I noticed you took Jose's gun."

"I did. He wasn't too pleased, but it was either take it or let him shoot me. It only has one full clip, though. If you happen to find a weapon or any extra ammunition, that would be awesome, too. Both of those men that passed us were carrying. If you can carry, too, it would even things up a bit."

He didn't look too pleased about the idea of shooting a gun at someone, but Whitney was trying to plan for any contingency. She wondered fleetingly what he was thinking. It was obvious that he wasn't happy about any of this, but he hadn't abandoned her, even though her presence had put him in a dangerous position. She was sorry about that, but she didn't see any options. Somehow, she would try to make it up to him, but right now wasn't the time or place to discuss it. She would dwell on that later—when she didn't have drug dealers trying to hunt her down and kill her.

They quickly boarded the separate boats and started searching. Whitney began by going through the compartments in the stern, then, finding nothing of value, headed for the hatches near the helm. She was pleasantly surprised to see the keys still in the ignition, and smiled to herself when she saw the cell phone tucked up into one of the small boxes. Both were an answer to prayer! Quickly pulling it out, she pushed the button to power on the device. The only thing that happened was the quick flash of the dead battery symbol on the screen before it disappeared. Whitney groaned. "Unbelievable."

"What's that?" Theo asked, glancing across at her from his position near the wheel of the larger boat.

"I found a cell phone, but the battery is dead. I guess that makes four times that Jose forgot to charge it, and I don't see a power cord anywhere, or a portable battery pack." She stowed the phone where it had come from. "How about over there?"

"Nothing so far," he responded.

"Jose left the keys. Wanna take this boat out for a spin?" She grinned just as the first shot slammed into the fiberglass only inches from her arm.

"Move again and the next one will be in your head."

Whitney's eyes flew to the end of the dock—and saw three men come out of the bushes, including Jose. They had moved much faster than she had expected, and now the two new arrivals were holding guns pointed directly at them. "Hands up," Shorty said roughly. "Slowly."

Whitney glanced over at Theo, who carefully raised his hands. Their eyes met for a moment, which was long enough for her to tell that he had some sort of plan up his sleeve. He glanced at the gun still secured in her waistband then back up into her eyes. Was he going to distract them so she could return fire? She locked eyes with him again and could see that he had confidence in her and her abilities, even though he had just met her. His support bolstered her resolve and she looked back at the dealers on the beach.

"Gentlemen, I'm so glad you decided to join us," she said brightly. "Turns out that I'm lost and I need a ride over to the mainland. Would you mind giving me a lift?"

Jose laughed. "Oh, we'll give you a ride, all right." He stepped on the wooden stairs leading to the dock just as Theo threw his backpack into the smaller boat and dove onto the floating dock and rolled, keeping low to the wood. The noise and movement were just what Whitney anticipated and made the perfect distraction. The larger man fired, but his shot went wild, while the other man's bullet hit the wooden post.

Whitney, on the other hand, was an excellent marksman, just as she'd previously claimed. Her first shot caught the larger man in the chest and he sank to the ground at the same time the smaller man's body fell beside him, also bleeding profusely from a bullet to the heart.

Jose turned and ducked, but Whitney was still able to catch him in the arm as he tried to scoop up the smaller man's gun. He shrieked in pain, but managed to keep a hold on the gun as he disappeared into the woods. Whitney fired once more, then decided to save her ammunition and focus on escape. Following after the man would be a mistake. She would be out in the open and, if he had any shooting ability at all, she would make an easy target.

She turned as she heard Theo untie the rope from the cleat on the dock, but kept the gun pointed at the woods, ready to fire if Jose engaged. Theo threw it into the boat and jumped in beside her. "Do you know how to drive one of these things?" she muttered, her eyes still narrowed on the shoreline.

"I sure do," he responded grimly.

"Then I think it's time we got out of here."

"Agreed," Theo said as he fired up the motor.

A few short minutes later, he was backing the boat away from the dock.

A bullet whizzed by Theo's head and he ducked instinctively, even as he heard Whitney return fire. He cleared the dock then pushed the throttle forward and relief swamped him as the boat quickly moved away from the dock and into the open water. Two more shots followed them, and although one hit the hull, the other missed completely. A few moments

As far as my pro-
with your first guess. I'm

more and he thought they were probably out of range of the drug dealer's pistol.

Theo's heart was pounding in his chest and he could feel the adrenaline coursing through his veins. He'd never been shot at before. *Ever.* God willing, he would never get shot at again, either. He was a scientist. He studied coral reefs. He glanced over at Whitney who looked perfectly at ease. She was probably used to being in the line of fire, but having people shoot at him took him way out of his comfort zone.

After a few minutes, Theo eased up a bit on the speed yet kept the boat pointed toward the mainland.

"Do you have a Coast Guard station anywhere around here?" Whitney asked as she flicked the safety on the gun and stored it in her waistband.

"There's one on Islamorada and one on Key West. There might be more, but those are the only ones I know about." He took a deep breath. "Key West is too far away, but we can get to Islamorada in a couple of hours. That's where they'd expect us to go, though." He grimaced. "When I was searching the bigger boat, I also found some rental papers in the hatch. It looks like they got that boat from a company out of Islamorada. If we go there, I'd imagine that they have the area covered." He shrugged, speaking the thoughts as they entered his mind. "Still, that's where the help is."

Whitney tossed her head to get some of the hair out of her eyes. "It's too bad we couldn't get one of those guy's phones. I know you didn't have service on the island, but hopefully we'll get somewhere eventually where we do." She pursed her lips then pressed on. "Look, I'm really sorry you got dragged into this. This is my problem, not yours. As soon as we get back to the mainland, I'll make sure you get to safety immediately. After a few days, hopefully you'll be able to pick up your life right where you left it."

He frowned. Was she serious? "I don't think you asked to be attacked by drug dealers on that boat yesterday, so I'm not sure you can classify it as 'your problem.'" He took off his glasses, cleaned the water away with his shirt and then put them back on, giving her a direct look. "Regardless, I think at this point it's *our* problem, don't you? Sure, they may have come after you initially, but after what just happened on my island, I believe we are both on their hit parade."

"I'm still sorry," she said again, her voice contrite.

As much as Theo wanted to blame her for their current situation, he found that he couldn't honestly lay the fault at her feet. Whitney had started this adventure by merely going on a wildlife cruise. She was supposed to be on vacation, and hadn't set out to wash up on his island. Or to be chased down by criminals.

He studied her face, which radiated a strong will and determination, and once again, he felt a spark of attraction toward her. Then, as he watched the wind play with her hair, his heart that had been beating with fear suddenly began pumping with an entirely new emotion that he refused to identify. He quickly looked away, trying to focus on driving the boat and [illegible] them. Why had God brought [...]he was a complication he just didn't need.

Sighing, he tried to push the sentiments away and stay focused on the conversation at hand.

"Thank you for saying so, but you're not responsible for any of this." He glanced at the sky, surreptitiously searching for a safe topic that would not make him think about Whitney Johnson's beautiful gray eyes. There was a storm building on the horizon. He had been tracking a storm in the Atlantic and mov[...] their way before all of this had happened. App[...] faster than the [...] to—which [...] stranger in his book—yet [...]erest was there. He couldn't think about her eyes even more. He groaned inwardly and searched for another subject. "So, you know I'm a biogeochemist, but I still don't know what you do for a living. Want to enlighten me?"

Whitney laughed. "I'll give you three guesses."

Theo grimaced. Her laugh was like music. He hadn't picked a safe topic, after all. He pushed forward. "Either a sharpshooter for the military," he said in a serious tone, "or a prison guard at a maximum-security facility. I still can't believe you bested Jose. That guy was huge!"

She laughed again, apparently pleased by both of his guesses. "Well, I grew up with three older brothers. I learned early on that I had to hold my own if they were going to take me seriously." She brushed some more hair out of her eyes. "▓▓▓▓▓▓▓ fession, you were closest w▓▓▓▓▓▓▓▓ a deputy US Marshal up in Tallahassee. There are two of us on the team that they call when they need a sharpshooter—either me or Jake Riley. We're about equal when it comes to accurately firing a weapon, not that the others on the team are slouches by any means. They keep Jake and me both on our toes."

Ah, everything about her was now starting to make more sense. The more he uncovered, the more the picture of Whitney Johnson came into focus. And Theo liked what he was discovering. She was not the typical female that he was attracted▓▓▓▓▓ made the entire situatio▓▓▓▓▓▓▓▓▓▓▓ he had to admit the int▓▓▓▓▓▓▓▓▓ explain his growing feelings, but he couldn't deny them, either.

Theo was never going to act on them, though. Attraction or not, losing his wife and child had devastated him. He never wanted to experience that type of pain again, and he would never willingly open himself up to that sort of vulnerability. Once this adventure was over, he would retreat to the solitude of his island and Whitney would return to Tallahassee, and their worlds would never again collide. That would be the end of it.

He was sure of it.

So why did that thought bother him so much?

SIX

The US Coast Guard station at Islamorada, which was smaller than Whitney expected, was housed on the end of a short peninsula. Theo piloted the boat up Snake Creek and turned right before the Overseas Highway drawbridge. As they pulled up, she noticed a T-shaped, two-story building that took up most of the space on the land, and a forty-five-foot Coast Guard Response Boat–Medium and a thirty-three-foot Special Purpose Craft Law Enforcement tied to the dock. There was room for another boat and Theo pulled into the space.

She didn't see any Coast Guard personnel around, but it was lunchtime, and it was a small station, so the lack of people wasn't too surprising. A large sign advertised the many missions of the station—to aid navigation, conduct search and rescue, marine environmental protection and, most important, drug and migrant interdiction.

A measure of relief swept over Whitney as Theo docked their boat. She'd never worked with the Coast

Guard directly, but if their sign was accurate, this was the perfect place to come for help from her plight with the drug dealers.

"So how many people work at this station?" she asked as Theo helped her out of the boat.

"A dozen or so, if I remember correctly," he answered. "I've only been here once and don't remember much about their setup."

"Hey, you can't leave your boat there," a voice called.

Whitney turned to see a young man in a navy blue uniform approaching. "We need some help," she said, her voice filled with authority. "I'm Whitney Johnson, US Deputy Marshal, and this is Theo Roberts."

The young man shrugged. "I don't care who you are. You can't leave your boat there. This dock is strictly off-limits to all except Coast Guard personnel. Captain Baker's orders, ma'am."

Whitney and Theo shared a look and Theo raised an eyebrow. Clearly, the name the young sailor had mentioned struck home with him, just as it did with Whitney. "Baker" was the name the drug dealer had mentioned on Theo's island. The implication had been that Baker was dirty. The last thing Whitney wanted to do was to jump from the fry pan and into the fire. Apparently, they would need to go elsewhere if they wanted help.

"And where can we find Captain Baker?" Theo asked.

The young man's eyes flitted over to Theo, giving both of them a suspicious look from head to toe. "Out on a mission, but he should be returning shortly, and he will want to dock his boat right where yours is now. A boat capsized just east of Plantation Key and he's out on the rescue. If you want to meet with him, I can contact him, set up an appointment and show you where to dock your boat so that it won't be in the way."

"That won't be necessary," Whitney stated flatly. "We're sorry to have bothered you. Do you think Captain Baker will be in tomorrow?" When the young man nodded, she smiled, hoping this entire event would be erased from his memory. The last thing she wanted to do was to bring any more attention to Theo or herself. At this point, she just wanted to get out of there before Baker heard about their visit and sent one of those large Coast Guard boats after them. If Captain Baker was corrupt, as she suspected, her life would be in even greater danger the moment he arrived. "Thanks for your help. We'll come back and go through official channels tomorrow. Sorry to have bothered you."

She and Theo both jumped back in the boat. As soon as Whitney untied it from the dock, he quickly pulled away from the small station and headed back out to sea.

Theo grimaced as they cleared the last of Snake Creek. "Well, that didn't work out so well."

"At least God protected us. If we'd showed up an hour later, Baker would have probably been there and who knows what would have happened." Whitney brushed some hair out of her eyes as the boat's speed picked up on the open water. "Got any other ideas?"

Theo shrugged. "It might be safer if we head into the Everglades. Doing the unexpected might just throw them off. Captain Baker is probably well respected in the area. Even local law-enforcement agencies in the vicinity will probably be looking for us on his say-so. I doubt it's safe to contact any of them."

"At this point, I just need a phone. I can call the Marshals in Tallahassee and get the protection we need."

"Well, I don't think it's safe to stop and try to find one anywhere around here, especially if Baker and that huge Coast Guard boat come back and chase us down." He grimaced. "There's no way we could outrun them in this little boat. I think what we need to do is put as much distance as we can between us and these drug dealers before we reach out for help."

Whitney sighed inwardly. Running and hiding wasn't usually the way she operated, but this was a new situation she had never faced before, and she had to think about Theo's safety as well as her own. "Any law enforcement in the Everglades besides the Fish and Wildlife Conservation Commission?"

He shook his head. "I doubt it, but those guys patrol on a regular basis. I don't know the towns along the Keys that well, but if these drug dealers are determined to find you and have a friend in Captain

Baker, they probably have the other Coast Guard stations already covered, too. I'm telling you, I really think our best bet is to head for the Everglades to see if we can find someone in authority who isn't influenced by the Coast Guard."

Whitney fisted her hands. She knew very little about the Everglades, but had avoided the area on purpose when she'd planned her vacation. "Is there anything in the Everglades besides alligators and more alligators?" she asked, hoping she was successfully keeping the trepidation out of her voice.

"Sure. They have mosquitos the size of horses." He looked over at her. "You have a problem with alligators?"

"Just when they try to eat me. That's all."

He grinned. "This from a woman who spent almost a whole day in the ocean and successfully avoided sharks for her entire swim?"

The smile warmed her. It was the first time she had seen Theo smile, and it lit his entire face. She liked the way his blue eyes shone with humor and crinkled in the corners, and how a dimple appeared in his left cheek. His expression made her feel like *anything* was possible. And, despite the circumstances, she found herself enjoying their playful banter. "Yeah, well, sharks don't seem quite as scary as those huge lizards with mouths full of teeth."

Theo laughed. "It's actually the other way around. Alligators are scared of humans. They will usually leave you alone unless you bother them. Sharks will swim up and take a bite, just to see if you taste good and to satisfy their curiosity."

"Why doesn't that thought make me feel any better?" she quipped. She glanced at Theo, who was expertly driving the boat. He looked totally at ease behind the wheel, and she liked the way the wind played with his hair. He was a good-looking guy. Scratch that. He was a *great*-looking guy. Yet it was obvious he wasn't looking for a relationship of any sort. Otherwise, why would he isolate himself on a deserted island in the Atlantic?

She cringed inwardly. It didn't matter anyway. After what the doctor had told her, no man would ever want to date her, let alone marry her. She had very little to offer with her current medical prognosis. She would end up alone, and at some point she would sit down and plot out a life for herself on this new road she was being forced to travel. She sighed and turned her thoughts to their current situation. She could figure out the rest later. Now wasn't the time or place to dwell on her problems.

"Do you know how to find help in the Everglades? I've never been there before."

"I know of a few research stations…that kind of thing," Theo replied. "There's a camping pavilion with some chickees I know about. We can stay there tonight, but it is no five-star hotel. After that, we'll probably have to start walking until we find a person with a phone." He seemed oblivious to the turmoil inside her, and Whitney was grateful that she had at least successfully hidden her distress from her companion. She had already brought danger to his life. She didn't want to involve him in her personal strife, as well.

Suddenly he motioned to her with his arm. "Get down! Quickly!"

Whitney immediately sank to the deck of the boat, her eyes filled with questions. Theo continued to look straight ahead as he drove, hoping he had gotten Whitney out of sight in time.

"There's a Coast Guard boat off to our left. It is still pretty far away, but I could see at least two of the seamen looking at our boat through binoculars. My guess is, the young sailor called Captain Baker and now he's on the lookout for two people fitting our description in a boat like this."

"Great," she responded, her voice filled with sarcasm. "Are they coming this way?"

"Not yet, but I'm going to—" He increased his speed. "I spoke too quickly. They're headed right for us." He had been moving toward the open sea from the Cotton Key Basin, but now he adjusted his course and turned back toward Plantation Key. They would be sitting ducks out in the open. There were a couple of other boats visible on the water, but not enough to effectively camouflage them, and the Coast Guard boat had much bigger engines and could overtake them in minutes with very little effort.

The boat turned smoothly at his direction and

Theo navigated carefully through Cowpens Cut, a narrow strip of water separating two small un-inhabited islands. He knew the Cut well and also knew it was commonly used by the locals as an easy way to return to Plantation Key. He glanced behind him. The Coast Guard boat was definitely follow-ing them, and was starting to gain ground. He had to do something to escape this new threat. His heart started beating against his chest like a bass drum, and adrenaline rushed through his veins. How had his life changed so drastically in such a short time? Yesterday morning he had been innocently running experiments in his lab. Today, he was on the run from the Coast Guard and a bunch of bloodthirsty drug dealers.

They made it through the Cut and Theo once again turned to look over his shoulder. The Coast Guard boat was still gaining on them and now he could see three or four men on the bow, all wearing the standard navy Coast Guard uniform. There was still a significant distance between the two boats, but Theo knew it couldn't last. It was only a matter of time before the larger boat overcame the smaller vessel.

"What's going on?" Whitney asked. She was still flat on the deck, trying to keep out of sight, but look-ing up at him, her steel-gray eyes were full of ques-tions.

Theo glanced down at her then back to where he was driving the boat. He imagined it was incredibly difficult for a woman of action like Whitney to be crouched on the floor of the boat, hiding. Still, he figured it was better if she stayed out of sight. "They're still following us and are gaining pretty quickly. Maneuvering into the Cut bought us a little time, but not enough. I give them ten minutes or so before they overtake us."

Instead of looking worried, a mask of determination settled across her features. "Do you have a plan?" she asked.

Whitney believed in him. He could see it in her eyes and the way she looked at him. The idea itself startled him. She didn't even really know that much about him, yet the look of confidence she gave him was staggering to say the least. In fact, he realized that she seemed to have more faith in him and his abilities than he did himself. Her strength bolstered his own, and he felt his spine stiffen and his own determination grow. He could do this. He'd been driving a boat since he was a teenager, and was well acquainted with how to handle a vessel in all sorts of situations.

"Actually, I do. There's a group of canals up here to the east. If we can make it there before they overtake us, we can try to hide in one of the boathouses."

"Works for me."

He made it into the canal that led to the Plantation Key marina, and slowed his speed to lessen his wake, trying his best not to do anything that would draw attention to either them or the boat they were using.

Suddenly they were passed by at least a dozen boats of various sizes, all heading in the opposite direction and out to the open sea. A sign on one of the boats advertised an armada race sponsored by the Coral Shores High School boating club, and most of the drivers were teenagers with a few parents sprinkled among the various boats for good measure. The boats not only clogged the canal, they also hid the boat Theo was driving as he continued down the waterway, looking for a good hiding place. The timing couldn't have been better, and he said a quick prayer of thanks. Maybe God was looking out for them, after all.

He quickly turned on the first canal to the right that he came across, still effectively blocked from view by the group of teenagers and their boats. The canal led into a crowded housing area, with dozens of boat docks and covered boat lifts.

He glanced behind him and saw no sign of the Coast Guard boat, which was probably still starting to maneuver into the mouth of the canal that led out to the ocean.

A large boathouse caught his attention to the left and he quickly noticed that it was empty. He pulled their boat in against the covered dock then quickly shut down the engine and jumped out of the boat.

Whitney started to stand but he waved her back down. "No, stay there. I'll be back in just a moment."

She followed his directions and waited where he'd left her, watching with interest as he rapidly tied off the boat then covered it with a blue tarp that had been rolled up and stored at the back of the boathouse. He dove back onto the boat and under the cover, just as he heard the telltale engine noise of the large Coast Guard vessel heading their direction down the canal.

His heart was still pumping madly as he landed next to Whitney and motioned with his hands for her to stay quiet.

A minute passed.

Then another.

He glanced into her eyes and was once again bolstered by the confidence he saw mirrored back at him. What possible reason could she have for giving him such unconditional support? Didn't she know that he didn't deserve her admiration? There were water droplets on his glasses and he took them off and looked away as he dried them, glad for something to do that would distract him from the beautiful woman beside him. He put them back on and was surprised when she reached out and took his hand, then squeezed it.

And she didn't let go.

In fact, she squeezed it harder as the rumble from the boat motor grew louder and louder as it approached. Her skin was soft like satin, and he reveled in the wonderful texture. He hadn't touched a woman in over four years, and the contact made him nervous yet delighted at the same time. How could a woman who'd bested and trussed up a large, burly drug dealer have hands as soft as rose petals? It didn't make sense.

They sat silently side by side, holding hands, waiting for the boat to pass. He sensed a vulnerability in her that he didn't expect. Whitney was so tough, so capable and so sure of herself. Here was yet another contradiction. Despite her abilities, she had sought comfort when he least expected it. He wasn't sure, but he almost felt like she was holding her breath. Or maybe that was him? Either way, the last thing he wanted to do was to pull away from her. He held her hand gently, glad to be able to lend her his strength.

The motor grumbled and seemed louder and louder with each passing second, and Theo closed his eyes and said another prayer. Were their pursuers going to notice them in the boathouse or pass them by?

SEVEN

The large Coast Guard boat motor seemed incredibly loud, and the sound rattled throughout Whitney's body. Her jaw started to ache from the way she was clenching her teeth, and she made a conscious effort to relax her facial muscles. She had a problem with dirty cops. Not long ago, her team of Marshals had worked with a man named Cassidy from the FBI. He had been on the take due to gambling debts. As a result, he had put all of their lives in danger, and one of the witnesses they were protecting had been shot and nearly killed.

To Whitney, being dirty on the job was the ultimate betrayal. There was a code the men and women who worked in law enforcement chose to live by and it included a large measure of trust and support, regardless of the patch worn on the officer's sleeve. Dirty cops violated that code. She didn't relish the idea of confronting Captain Baker without proof, but she would do so if she had to, even if it cost her dearly.

The last thing she wanted, though, was to drag Theo Roberts into the brawl. By all appearances, he was a handsome, well-educated and thoughtful scientist who cared deeply about the world around him. And Whitney could tell there was even more to this wonderful man bubbling just below the surface of his calm veneer, waiting to be discovered.

Theo had been hurt. By something or someone. He was an introvert, that was obvious, but his behavior went beyond that endearing personality trait. Apparently the scars ran so deep that his answer had been to seclude himself on a deserted island, and to inundate himself with the kind of work that kept his mind occupied and prevented him from dwelling on whatever had happened. He had been a doctor, sworn to help others, yet he had turned his back on that profession. What could possibly have happened to make him choose such a drastic life change?

She had no clue what hurt Theo was hiding from, but she was an expert at reading people, and his pain was nearly palpable. She did not want him mixed up in this huge mess that she currently found herself in. It wasn't fair to him. She also didn't want to add to the misery he was already experiencing. So she sat there, holding on for dear life, hoping that the Coast Guard boat would pass them by without Theo suffering any further because of her.

A moment passed.

Then another.

The Coast Guard's boat passed them by and she

blew out a relieved breath as the sound of the motor grew more and more distant. They were safe for now, but what she really needed was a place to hide where she could contact her team and get their assistance without endangering anybody else. She knew she could trust her team, but she couldn't say the same for the local law-enforcement crew. Surely most of them were dedicated officers who took their oaths seriously. But she didn't have any way to distinguish between those officers and the ones influenced by Captain Baker. Nor did she have the time to figure it out before the drug dealers were once again breathing down their necks.

Once she no longer heard the boat motor, she gave Theo's hand a final squeeze and stood, pushing aside the tarp as she did so. "Ready to head for the Everglades?"

"Still seems like the safest plan to me," he agreed as he helped her to fold and stow the tarp back where he'd found it.

They waited a few more minutes, just to make sure their pursuers were truly gone, then Theo steered the boat out of the slip and in the direction of the way they'd come. A short time later, they were on the open ocean, once again headed for the Everglades. The Coast Guard boat was nowhere in sight.

"Ready for something to eat?" Theo asked once it was clear that nobody was following them.

"Sure," Whitney responded. "What have you got to offer?"

"There's some fruit and other goodies in my back-pack. I grabbed a few things before we left the island this morning."

She found his backpack and pulled out the bag of fruit as they headed north. "So what's your plan after we arrive at the Everglades?"

Theo smiled as he took a piece of mango that she offered. Had he noticed that she had homed in again on the pineapple? She truly loved the fresh taste, and was devouring piece after piece that had been in the bag.

He took a bite and turned his attention back to expertly maneuvering the boat. "There are some chickees in the backcountry that are used by scientists doing extended research in the area. They apply and get permits issued by the government, and then they can stay for a small fee and use the facilities while they work. The huts are pretty rustic, but not very many people know about them. I'm hoping we can head in that direction and find someone staying there that has a phone. Then we can stay with them until your team arrives." He glanced at her. "That is your plan, right? Call your Marshals, so you'll be able to get help from the people you trust?"

She nodded. "I definitely want to call my team, but if we can't, I'm hoping we run across some of those Fish and Wildlife folks you mentioned. Maybe they're far enough removed from the Coast Guard crew to be safe. You said they patrol the park regularly. If that's the case, they can probably help us sooner than the Marshals can get here, if we think we can trust them. I'm just nervous about working with anyone locally in the Keys. I don't know how long Captain Baker's reach might be."

Theo finished off the first mango chunk and she handed him another. He raised his eyebrow when he noticed she wasn't sharing the pineapple, but gave her a smile. She reluctantly handed him a piece of the yellow fruit when she noticed his expression, and he laughed outright. "And what if the FWC folks do have ties to Baker and his drug-dealing friends?"

She ate her piece of fruit, thinking through the possibilities. "You make a valid point. It's a risk, and I am out of my element here. I don't know who I can trust and who I can't. The safest thing to do is to contact my team first and let them take the lead, but we might not have that option. If we're able to reach them, though, they can contact the Miami office and start the investigation from there." She looked him in the eye. "Still, our first priority is getting you to safety."

Theo frowned. "*Me?* What do you mean? Why not the both of us?"

Whitney shrugged. "Look, this kind of life is what I signed up for. You didn't. In law enforcement, our primary objective is keeping civilians safe. The last thing I want is for you to get hurt because of me, especially after you've done so much to help me."

"Just because I'm not law enforcement, doesn't mean I'm going to abandon you the first chance I get." A muscle ticked in his jaw. "If that were the case, we could have left the boat in that neighborhood in Plantation Key and gone our separate ways. I'm in this for the duration until we are both safe."

Whitney looked into his sea-blue eyes and saw the truth behind his words. A warm feeling invaded her chest and seeped all the way down to her toes. They both knew instinctively that abandoning the boat in that neighborhood would have been a mistake. It would only have been a matter of time before the Coast Guard or the local police would have found them, and neither one of them knew how much influence Baker had over the locals.

Still, Theo would have had a better chance of blending into the woodwork and returning to his own life if he'd left her to survive on her own. And she *would* have struggled. Even she had to admit that. Whitney sighed. She had no idea how to drive a boat, even though she was willing to learn, and she wasn't familiar with this area where everyone seemed to know everyone. She was a city girl from a totally different part of the state, and was happier behind a computer or on the shooting range than she was skimming over the ocean.

"Thank you for staying." The words were hard for her to say on a couple of different levels. She was a very capable woman and didn't like to depend on anyone else outside of her team of US Marshals. Especially when being threatened. She also had come to the Keys for solitude so she could ponder her choices and determine her next course since the life she had previously planned was no longer an option.

Still, the words were heartfelt. Whitney was glad Theo was with her. She didn't quite understand him, and he was not the usual type of man that she found attractive, yet there was something that drew her to him all the same. She liked his strong yet gentle demeanor and the sweetness in his smile. He was like a harbor in a storm—safe, secure and rock-solid. Even though she had only known him a short time, she knew for a fact that he would do anything he could to protect her. He was just that kind of man.

She offered him the last piece of mango and he grinned in return and accepted it. "You're welcome. You've definitely added some spice to my life." He gave her a playful nudge and she nudged him back, enjoying the camaraderie and peaceful moment, unsure if they would find the safety they were seeking in the day ahead. She didn't know much about the area, but everything she'd heard about the Everglades made her think of alligators, swamps and twenty-foot snakes. None of that sounded any good to her.

Theo continued to drive the boat, lost in thought as Whitney made herself comfortable in the seat next to him. He watched as she fished the bottle of aloe out of the backpack and started applying it to her skin.

Try as he might, he couldn't explain the emotions he was experiencing. His life had been in constant peril since he'd met Whitney, yet he was feeling more alive than he had since he had moved onto his quiet little island. And when he'd had the opportunity to let her go—he had held on fast. Why? He didn't want a relationship. Hadn't he already determined that?

Theo wanted to go back and continue his life as before—without the threat of drug dealers trying to kill him. He had his experiments and the journal article he was in the middle of writing that still needed some work. Yet the thought of returning right now was unappealing, and it was all due to this woman sitting beside him.

He wanted to know more. Who was Whitney Johnson? Maybe that was it. After his curiosity was satisfied—and once he knew she was safe—then he could go back.

"So, what drew you into law enforcement?" Theo asked, taking a drink from his water bottle. He might as well learn more about her if they were going to be spending time together. Or at least, he tried to convince himself that was his only motivation as he piloted the boat toward the Everglades.

She got her own water bottle and unscrewed the cap. "Family history. I have three brothers who are all in various law-enforcement agencies, and my dad was a cop, so that's pretty much all we talked about growing up. I'm the youngest of the bunch, and my brothers tried to point me in a different direction, but how could I let them have all the fun?"

"Fun?" Surprised, he hoped he successfully kept

"I was an ER doctor in Tampa, but I…had some setbacks and decided to go a different direction." *Had some setbacks?* The words seemed frozen on his tongue. His wife and daughter had died, and he had just minimized the entire accident by calling it a setback. He tried again, but couldn't seem to form the words. The past was the past. He didn't want to discuss it ever again. It was too painful. Just thinking about it brought up his own feelings of failure and inadequacy. "I'd rather not talk about it. The work I'm doing now with the coral is important. The coral reefs are dying, and they're vital to the ecosystem here. I'm trying to figure out what is harming the staghorn coral in particular, and how to regenerate it so we can rebuild the reefs."

Whitney seemed to take his comments and attitude in stride. Theo was grateful she didn't press. "So is your work associated with one of the state universities?"

"I'm coordinating my efforts with a team from Florida State University, but my work is funded by a federal grant."

Whitney motioned with her arm and did the Seminole chop. "Ah, so you are a Florida State Seminole. I can spot a fellow Seminole a mile away."

Theo laughed. The in-state rivalry was fierce between the two top state universities—Florida State and the University of Florida. Both schools inspired a great deal of loyalty. "So what was your major at FSU—criminal justice?"

"Actually, that was my minor—my major was computer science."

"So, when my computer crashes, you're the one to call?"

"Absolutely." Whitney grinned.

Her gentle good humor started to creep back into the conversation, and Theo knew that he couldn't stay dwelling on the past. Not only couldn't—he found that he didn't want to stay in the past. What he wanted and needed was to be in the here and now so he could help Whitney survive this challenge. This trial was testing him, as well, and his heart was beating with renewed vigor as he navigated the crystal blue water that surrounded them. All they had to do now was to survive and escape into the Everglades. How hard could that be?

EIGHT

"Hello! Anyone home?"

Theo idled the motor and slowly approached the chickees. There was a large, two-person kayak tied to the metal ladder that led to the sheltered platform, which was surrounded by water, and there was a standalone tent set up in the middle of the platform. A wooden deck led from the chickee to the beach, and another deck walkway led to a small bathroom off to the left. Another empty chickee was also a stone's throw away and connected by yet another wooden walkway.

Theo pulled up next to the kayak and stopped the motor, then threw the rope up to Whitney, who tied the boat off on one of the hut's support beams.

"Are you sure there isn't a ranger station anywhere nearby?" she asked. "I hate to bother these folks and draw them into this mess."

"Not that I remember," Theo confirmed. "These huts can be rented at the Flamingo ranger station, but that's still pretty far away. I think there was a marina near the ranger station where a person could rent a canoe or kayak, but I'm not positive. It's been a while since I've been here, and I'm not too sure anymore. I think there is also a pavilion of some sort on land, back on the beach behind those trees." He pointed toward the land. "These mangrove waterways seem to stretch on forever and are like a maze back here, and lots of times, people get lost in the backcountry and the rangers have to come find them. Hopefully, whoever's camping here can help us out when they return and point us in the right direction."

Whitney pulled on the ladder to draw the boat closer, then suddenly let out a shriek and yanked her hand back.

Theo responded instantly and moved to her side, then took her hand. "I don't see any marks. What happened?"

"I touched something slimy. It could have been a frog. Whatever it was moved and surprised me."

Theo laughed. "The Everglades are filled with wildlife, and there are all kinds of birds and bugs back here, not to mention the lizards, snails and frogs you'll find."

Whitney pulled her hand away and gave him a look. "Not to mention the alligators with mouthfuls of teeth and the venomous snakes. Let's not forget them."

Theo immediately replaced his laugh with a contrite expression, but he couldn't keep the smile from his lips. After everything that had happened in the last day or so, it was nice to find something to laugh about. It was also interesting to see a crack in Whitney's armor. She was one tough cookie, but she was finally starting to let down her guard around him— even if just for a moment. He was intrigued, and couldn't keep the question in. "You mean, you'll take down a vicious drug dealer that is twice your size without a second thought, but you can't touch a frog without screaming?"

"Something like that," Whitney conceded as she wiped her hand on her shorts. Apparently she noticed his raised eyebrow and incredulous look, and decided to give him an explanation. "Look, I don't do outdoors, okay? I was born and raised in Atlanta. You know, home of the Olympics and the fourteen-lane highway? I stayed away from bugs and frogs and anything else that was slimy to the best of my ability my entire life."

"But you were on a wildlife tour boat when you started this journey, weren't you?"

"Yes. The kind where the guide points to the wildlife and I say, 'Wow, that's pretty,' take a picture with my phone, and then we move on to the next. Then, after a few hours of sunbathing, I return to my hotel and eat a nice meal. That's what I signed up for. I didn't plan on interacting with or touching anything creepy along the way." As if to accent her point, a dragonfly buzzed near her head and she swatted it away. "This trip is getting worse by the moment."

"We'll be fine if we can find the owner of this

tent. Hopefully, they'll be back soon and we can borrow this kayak. It looks like it will fit two people and even has a storage bin where we can put the backpack."

"Why don't we take it now?" Whitney asked as she studied the kayak. "The water looks too shallow to take the boat any further, but with this kayak, we might be able to make it to the trailhead and a ranger station. We can leave a note, and I'll be sure to pay them back for the loan of the kayak once we find the owners."

"Two reasons," Theo answered. "First, I don't know this area that well and we need a map to help us navigate through the mangroves. And second, there's no paddle in the kayak, and I don't see an extra one anywhere in the chickee. Looks like there are two people staying here, and they must be out and about in another boat or canoe, with the paddles. We won't get far without at least one paddle to help us steer."

There was a small splash near the beach and both Whitney and Theo turned to see a six-foot alligator swimming toward them.

"Good grief!" Whitney said frantically as she grabbed the ladder once again and pulled herself up onto the platform. "Can it get up here?"

"I doubt it. I think it was probably sunning itself on that log over there. Our talking probably scared it."

"Then why is it coming straight at us?"

They watched for a moment, and even though the

alligator had started in their direction, it suddenly ducked below the surface and disappeared.

"I imagine it was curious, but then got distracted. It probably just found dinner. There are a lot of fish around here. It likely just grabbed a meal and is heading back home to enjoy it. You don't need to worry. Like I said before, they're more scared of us than we are of them."

"Don't be so sure about that," Whitney responded.

Theo smiled and followed her up the ladder. They looked through the windows of the tent. There were two sleeping bags inside, a couple of pillows and two large backpacks. A box of supplies sat near the zippered entrance, along with a small cooler, but that was about it. Outside the tent, two towels had been slung over a rafter to dry, and there was a collection of small aquariums protected by a fabric sun shield that let air through but kept the aquariums in shadow, presumably to keep them cool in the August heat. Each one had a wire-mesh lid and grasses on the bottom. A second and larger cooler was under the towels, as well as a couple of plastic containers filled with papers and small notebooks. Theo opened the largest of the containers and found a laptop and a fancy camera.

"What do you think you're doing?" The male voice was angry, and came at them from a shout across the bay.

"Get out of our chickee!" a second voice yelled.

This angry male voice was much less forceful than the first.

Theo let the container lid shut by itself and slowly turned, keeping his hands spread and up in a motion of surrender. He didn't want the newcomers to feel threatened in any way. For all he knew, they had a gun and would take a shot at him if he moved.

"We didn't mean to intrude," Whitney said, her voice small. "We were just looking for a phone."

Theo was so surprised by her tone that he swung his head in her direction, his eyebrows raised. Who was that meek, mousy girl that had just spoken? Gone was the impressive, tough, law-enforcement agent. Even her posture had changed. What was her game? He barely recognized her.

The two men continued their approach, the man in the stern of the canoe paddling furiously until they pulled up beside the kayak. A few minutes later, the first man was on the platform, standing only inches away from Theo, his posture threatening.

"You want to explain to me what you're doing rooting through our supplies?"

Theo didn't back down and stood his ground, despite the man's irate tone. In fact, he found it interesting that the man was totally ignoring Whitney, which was probably what she had hoped for with her submissive demeanor. Pretending to be a helpless female was an effective tool in her toolbox. He wondered how many people she had fooled with the act. Probably several.

The newcomer was a large man with tanned, leathery skin and a head of curly dark hair. He also had a scruffy beard beginning on his cheeks and chin. He probably hadn't shaved for a week or more, which gave him an even more roguish appearance. If Theo had to guess, he imagined the man was in his late twenties or early thirties. It was more than the man's disheveled appearance that worried Theo, however. The large man's hands were fisted as if he was about to take a swing at him.

Theo did his best to stay calm, modulating his voice and making sure his stance was not threatening in any way. They'd already survived their encounter with drug dealers and flying bullets on the island, and being chased by the Coast Guard cruiser. If they were thoughtful and deliberate with their actions, they could survive this confrontation with the campers, as well. "Like the lady said, we were just looking for a phone. We had some problems out on the water, and were looking to contact a ranger and get some help."

Theo glanced over at Whitney. The newcomer still hadn't paid her much attention, but Theo saw the light in her eyes and the way she held herself. He could tell she was like a firecracker, just waiting to explode into motion if necessary. It was interesting that he was already learning subtle things about her and could read her expression so easily.

He returned his focus to the angry man in front of him, then took a step back, his hands still up. "We didn't mean any harm, sir." He looked over the man's shoulder to the other guy, who was still in the canoe. The man's face was rather pale, despite the tanned skin, and he was holding himself as if he were in pain. "Is your friend okay?"

"He's fine," the man replied. "Take your girlfriend and get out of here. We've got a permit and have this whole area reserved for the next three days."

Theo looked around the aggressive dude's shoulder, trying to get a better look at the man in the canoe. It was hard to get a good look from this angle and with the man before him trying to block his view. Still, he could see the pain etched on the second fellow's face. "He doesn't look fine. He looks hurt. I'm a doctor. Can I help?"

"Yeah, sure you are." The man's voice held a mixture of derision and hopefulness at the same time as he looked him over from head to toe.

"He *is* a doctor." Whitney spoke up, her act of appearing helpless suddenly forgotten. Theo was amazed that she could change her stance so quickly. Perhaps she sensed, as he did, that the threat had dissipated. Now a tough US Marshal stood on the platform, and when she spoke, her voice held a tone of authority. "You should let him take a look at your friend. He might be able to help."

The curly haired man fisted and unfisted his hands, apparently considering their words. A moment passed. Then another. Finally, he made a decision and took a step back, motioning to the man in the boat as he did so. "You'd better not be lying."

"Good grief," Whitney said roughly as she pushed by him, giving him a look as she did so. "You're over here posturing while your friend is hurt? What kind of friend are you?" The man's eyes widened as she shoved him aside.

Theo shrugged and followed her to the edge of the platform, trying his best to keep his mirth from showing. He'd already decided never to cross Whitney when she was in law-enforcement mode. Apparently this stranger had just learned the same lesson.

Theo descended the ladder and pulled the canoe closer, then got in the boat. The man had a towel wrapped around his upper arm, and it was stained with fresh blood. Theo gingerly removed the towel and saw several gashes in his arm, accented by three or four puncture marks. All were bleeding rather badly. "My name is Theo Roberts, and I really am a doctor despite the fact that I look like I'm on vacation," he said as he examined the wounds. "What's your name?"

"John Pierce. That's my brother, Mark." He nodding at the curly haired man. "We're out here studying the pythons in the Glades."

"No python made these wounds," Theo observed as he conducted a thorough examination.

John shook his head. "You're right. This is an alligator bite. Unfortunately, I put my arm where it didn't belong."

Whitney raised an eyebrow. "Did I just hear you say you got bitten by an *alligator*?"

"It wasn't the alligator's fault," John quickly supplied. "She was defending her nest. I just didn't realize her nest was there until the last moment. Then it was too late."

"Alligators usually aren't aggressive unless they feel threatened," Mark stated tightly, as if he were in a classroom. "They are naturally afraid of people. This was John's mistake, not hers."

"Well, we need to get this wound cleaned up." Theo wrapped the towel back around the man's arm to help stanch the bleeding. "Alligators have bacteria in their mouths, just like most creatures. You also are going to need a few stitches." He looked over at Whitney, who's face had an expression that said *I told you so* quite clearly. He shook his head and gave her a good-natured wink.

"I don't think I can get out of this canoe by myself," John said tightly. "This arm really hurts."

"We'll help you," Whitney told him. "Let's get you up here on the chickee."

Between the three of them, they were able to help John get up on the platform. Thankfully, Mark was also able to produce a first-aid kit and a bottle of hydrogen peroxide.

Theo immediately went to work cleaning the injured man's wounds.

Whitney was fascinated as she watched Theo work. It was so evident that he had a gift with helping people. Why had he given up practicing medicine to study coral reefs on an isolated island in the Florida Keys? It was still a mystery, but one she hoped she would be able to solve before they parted ways. It just didn't make sense for a man who was so clearly talented to turn away from his chosen profession.

Theo was gentle, like always, yet each motion was exact and practiced, and his tone was calm as he distracted his patient with questions while he worked.

"So you are a biologist?"

"Yes, we both are," John replied. "We're doing a study for the University of Florida on the pythons that are taking over the Glades."

"Over the past ten years, all sorts of exotic snakes have been showing up in the Everglades," Mark interjected. "People buy them as pets and they become either too big or too expensive to care for. Then they bring them out here and release them. The Burmese python is the most problematic, so we're trying to get a handle on the best way to find and humanely remove them. The alternative is the python hunts they have each year all over South Florida. The Feds have been trying to find ways to increase access to remote areas in the Everglades. Then they hire python hunters to go in and remove the snakes."

"Pythons eat all sorts of other animals," his brother added. "They aren't choosy at all, which is probably why there has been such a sharp decline in the number of mammals here. Those snakes are devastating the entire ecosystem." He shrugged. "The Fish and Wildlife Conservation Commission has an Exotic Pet Amnesty Program that allows people to surrender the snakes without penalty. I wish more people would take advantage of it."

Whitney shivered involuntarily and motioned toward the aquariums that were stacked under the sun shade. "Are you telling me those containers are filled with snakes?"

"Pretty much," Mark added with a smile, clearly enjoying making the tough lady squirm with his words. "They're little snakes, though, not the huge ones you see in the jungle documentaries. A few crates have lizards in them. Don't worry, we have collection permits. I promise."

John grimaced as Theo began stitching his arm with a small kit he'd found in the first-aid box. "We were mapping a particularly large python when my foot got tangled in some underwater brush. I reached down to free my foot, and the next thing I know, the alligator bit my arm."

Whitney's eyes rounded. "You were walking in this water? Are you *nuts*?"

"We were wearing boots and waterproof pants to keep the bugs out. Even the boots couldn't have stood up to the alligator's teeth, though, if she'd wanted to take a bite. I'm lucky it was just my arm that she bit."

"I'd say," Mark agreed.

"I'm also lucky that she wasn't hungry. If she had been, she would have held on longer and tried to pull me down into the water and take me for a roll. This was just a warning bite to stay away from her nest."

Theo finished stitching and started to wrap the

wounds with gauze. "Well, that should do it. Don't get this arm wet for a week or so. Do you have a way to keep it protected?"

"I'll figure something out," John replied. "Thanks for taking care of me."

Theo nodded. "You're welcome."

Whitney glanced at the sky. "I don't relish spending the night out here, but it's already late afternoon and it looks like a storm might be rolling in. Those clouds to the east have been looking rather ominous all day. Do you think we can make it to the nearest ranger station before dark?"

John shook his head. "We're a good three hours away from the closest station. Your best bet is to wait until morning. You'll get lost in the mangroves if you start back now." He glanced at the sky. "I heard the weather report yesterday about a tropical storm in the Atlantic, but most of the models have it going up the east coast without giving us much besides a little rain. They don't think it's going to turn into a hurricane, but you never know. We'll probably go back early if the weather doesn't improve."

He stretched out his injured arm and wiggled his fingers, then winced but smiled through the pain. "I can't tell you how thankful we are that you came along when you did. I sure am glad you were able to patch me up. Can we do anything to pay you back?"

"We'd love to borrow your phone, if you have one," Whitney said.

"No phone," John told her regretfully. "There's no

internet out here, of course, but we were using the phone as a hotspot so we could share our notes with our colleagues back at the university. Mark didn't even bring his phone. He's antitechnology."

Mark scowled. "I'm a Luddite. That's not the same."

John laughed but continued. "Well, this morning, I accidently crushed my phone as we were heading out. It fell out of my pocket and I stepped on it as I was carrying a heavy box. Stupid mistake on my part, but the thing is well and truly ruined." He pulled it out of his pocket and showed them the damaged screen that was covered with cracks. "The thing won't even turn on anymore. We have solar chargers for it, but it won't hold a charge. Looks like I'll be forced to buy a new one once we get back to town."

"Not one of our brightest moments," Mark agreed.

"Well, you are Florida Gators…" Whitney gibed, a grin on her face as she hinted at the college rivalry between the University of Florida and the Florida State University. "After all, your mascot is the gator, and here you are, getting bitten by one and destroying your phone all in the same day…"

"Hey now," Mark said, a mock frown on his face. "Don't tell me you're a Seminole?" he said lightly, mentioning the FSU mascot. The in-state enmity between the two schools was legendary. "I was actually starting to like you, but now I'm not so sure…"

"If you don't have a working phone, would you mind if we borrowed your kayak to get to the ranger station?" Theo interjected, stopping the college rivalry discussion before it got out of hand. "I think Whitney is right. There is a storm brewing."

She smiled as he deftly changed the subject. It was clear that Theo was in business mode, trying to solve their problems. She liked that he was a planner, thinking three steps ahead, whereas she usually lived in the here and now. It was refreshing to be around someone with a personality that was so different from her own. And he was right. The first order of business was getting them somewhere safe and away from the drug dealers, not joking around with two biologists.

Whitney sighed. She had already dragged him away from his home and put him in danger on multiple occasions. Of course he was anxious to solve their problems and return to the island as soon as possible. She turned her attention to the issue at hand.

"It's really important that we get to a phone as soon as possible. We can leave you the boat, if you can use it and you want to return to the mainland sooner than later. It's a rental and eventually has to be returned to Plantation Key, but I'd imagine that any marina could take care of that for us."

"Why don't you just use the boat to go back the way you came?" John asked, his voice suddenly laced with suspicion.

"That's simply not possible," Theo answered. "And you're better off not knowing why, believe me."

Mark took a step forward. "Are you two in some kind of trouble?"

NINE

"I'm a Deputy US Marshal," Whitney stated, her tone matter-of-fact. "I'm working on a case, and Theo is helping me. That's all I'm really at liberty to say."

"Do you have a badge I can see?" Mark asked.

Whitney shook her head. "This whole thing started while I was on vacation. My badge and gun are at home."

She watched as Mark and John shared a look then seemed to come to an agreement, even without having a conversation out loud. Suspicious or not, they were apparently grateful for the medical service Theo had performed, and were willing to help them out without pushing for more details to assuage their curiosity. Since Whitney and Theo were running to the ranger station and not away from the FWC, the brothers probably also believed that their guests hadn't broken the law or done some other nefarious deed, despite her lack of credentials.

Mark finally shrugged. "We don't need your boat,

but thanks for the offer. We can fit everything back in the canoe when it's time to go, but for now, we're going to stay and finish our research—unless that storm keeps growing."

John looked Theo in the eye. "I don't know what kind of trouble you're in, but you should know, the rangers do patrol this area on occasion. You might be lucky enough to run into one on the way tomorrow. Keep an eye out. As far as the boat goes, the guys from the marina also know the area. We could leave it here. You would just need to report it when you get to the ranger station."

"It's too shallow to use in these waters anyway," Mark agreed.

Whitney was relieved that the boat wasn't an issue. They still had to find a phone, of course, and get to safety. But boats were expensive, and even though the drug dealers had rented the boat in the first place and were ultimately responsible for it, she doubted they cared what happened to it. Still, she didn't want the marina owners to lose out on thousands of dollars just because they had unwittingly rented the boat to criminals.

John and Mark shared another look and then Mark motioned toward the kayak. "As for the kayak, yeah, you can take it. John's not going to be paddling anytime soon anyway, and we can get by with the canoe. All we ask is that you leave it at the marina by the ranger station at the trailhead. That way we'll get our deposit back on our credit card. In the meantime, let us feed you a nice meal tonight, and we'll point you in the right direction come morning."

"Yeah," John added as he rubbed his injured arm above the wounds. "It's too late to be heading back now anyway. You'd end up paddling in the dark. It's hard enough to navigate these waterways when you can see where you're going. You'll get lost for sure if you try to do it at night."

Whitney looked over at Theo, who nodded. "Deal," she agreed. She didn't like the idea of staying another night out here without finding a phone, but it seemed as if they had little choice. At least they had a plan for the morning. She slapped at a mosquito. "You wouldn't happen to have any bug spray, would you?"

"We're loaded with it, although we're lucky. We haven't needed it as much as we thought we would. The breeze flows pretty well down here and sweeps most of them away from the chickees." He pointed to one of the storage bins. "There's a bottle in there. Help yourself."

She found the bottle and slathered it on her skin, then passed it to Theo, who also applied it. Breeze or not, she didn't need any more problems with her skin. The sunburn was already bad enough.

The two brothers fixed a nice meal, preparing some fish they'd caught earlier, as well as some other food they had packed in. Fire wasn't allowed, but gas stoves were, and the two had apparently made eating well during a camping trip into an art form.

Whitney hadn't realized how hungry she was until she started to sample their offerings. All she'd had today was a couple of muffins and some fruit. Once she started, however, she couldn't seem to stop. She thought back to what she'd eaten over the last couple of days and realized the meals had been rather sparse. There had just been so much going on that it had been hard to even think about food. But now she and Theo were both relaxed and felt relatively safe for the time being. A good meal with new friends was the perfect way to enjoy the evening. *Even if they are Florida Gators*, she amended to herself.

After they'd all eaten their fill and cleaned up after the meal, they left John to rest and Mark, Theo and Whitney paddled both the kayak and the canoe over to the beach. They pulled the canoe up onto the sand. Then the three of them carried the kayak over to another area about five hundred feet from the bay where there was a small dock that led into the mangroves.

Whitney noticed a state park sign posted by the dock that gave some background information about the area and the surrounding wildlife. There was also a map of the canoe trails carved into the wood. Painted green, there was a big red X that proclaimed "You are here." It looked like a child had drawn a maze on the map, with the X on one end of the game and the ranger station at the other. How were they ever going to find their way out of this mess? she wondered as Theo joined her in front of the signpost.

"It's not as confusing as it seems," Mark reassured them as he noticed their apprehension. He pointed to a wooden stake driven into the ground, the top of which was painted red. Apparently he was a mind reader as well as a biologist. "The trail is marked, but some of the signs are hard to find. Just keep a lookout for the red markers. Some people do get lost back here, but it's usually because they're just not paying attention. Are you sure you don't want to just go back with your boat to one of the Keys?"

"We're sure," Whitney and Theo said together as one and then laughed, despite the seriousness of the situation. The drug dealers were near. She could feel it. And they couldn't go back. Their only hope was to escape into the park and evade their pursuers until they could find a phone and call for help from someone they trusted.

"We sure appreciate you allowing us to take the kayak," Theo added. He was standing extremely close to Whitney and she could hear his breathing and felt a whisper of it against the back of her neck. Her first instinct was to step away, but she didn't. In fact, despite her toughness, she found his presence calming and reassuring. Both feelings were oddly surprising to her, but she couldn't deny they existed. She was out of her element and it was good to have someone nearby that knew a thing or two about how to survive in the outdoors.

"Are you sure you can do without it?" she asked, stepping back to the kayak.

Mark shrugged. "We'll be fine. We're almost done out here anyway and, like you said, there seems to be a storm brewing. After a couple more days, we'll be packed up and ready to go, unless John's injuries start to bother him and we need to leave sooner." He smiled. "Besides, you two seem to need it more than we do."

"Thanks for everything you've done," Whitney acknowledged. She leaned over and checked the kayak one last time to make sure all was ready for them to slide it into the water the next day and be on their way. It seemed simple enough, but she'd never paddled a boat before. She hoped Theo knew how to steer the thing. Straightening, she rubbed her belly, once again thankful for the food. It was amazing how much better she felt now that her stomach was full. "That was an amazing meal. Do you guys always eat that well?"

"Not always." Mark laughed. "It depends upon what fish we can catch. Our permit is very specific and only allows us to harvest certain fish. Sometimes, the right ones just aren't biting." He pointed into the woods. "I have a surprise for you. There's a small building back there where you can sleep tonight. It's not much—just like a little gazebo that people use for teaching, resting off the trail, that sort of thing. Still, it's screened, which will keep the majority of the bugs away. And it has a bathroom. John still has his hammock in there I think, and I'm sure he won't mind if you use it."

They followed him along a narrow trail that led away from the bay, and suddenly came upon a small building that was partially hidden by the trees.

They entered and Whitney glanced around. There wasn't much to it, but three of the walls were solid wood, and the other three were screened in, so it offered some shelter from the elements and the bugs, just as Mark had suggested. There was a desk and a chair, along with three wooden benches, and that was the extent of the furniture. A broom stood in the corner and it was evident that someone had recently swept the floor and also knocked down the cobwebs from the corners. Overall, it was relatively clean, despite the rustic appearance. Mark took the towel from around his neck and handed it to her.

"Sorry, I don't have a blanket, but this towel will keep away the chill, at least a little bit." He motioned around the room. "Are you sure you'll be okay tonight in here by yourself? John and I won't bother you, I promise, and there is still that other chickee out on the bay that would probably be more comfortable for you. We could rig the hammock up out there for you instead if you're interested."

Whitney shook her head, grateful for the hammock and the screened-in building that would offer her some measure of privacy. Theo must have explained to the two biologists at some point that they weren't married and needed separate sleeping quarters, and she was thankful for that, as well. She also felt safer in here than she did out in the open where the alligators and snakes called home.

"I'll take the other chickee," Theo said mildly, apparently reading her thoughts. "I think Whitney wants these screens to keep the bugs away, and I'll enjoy the breeze."

Whitney nodded, relieved that they were on the same page. "This is perfect. Thank you." She hoped that between the breeze and the bug spray, the insects wouldn't be too bad for him during the night.

"I've got to check something. I'll meet you by the canoe on the beach." Mark said his goodbyes and left, leaving Theo behind.

Whitney raised an eyebrow and Theo shrugged as he watched Mark disappear down the trail. He turned back to Whitney, a contrite expression on his face. "Well, that wasn't very subtle. Sorry about that. He still thinks I'm your boyfriend, despite what I told him. I guess he was trying to give us a chance to say good-night in private." He had his hands on his hips and looked like he was about to say something else. Then he stopped and shook his head as if disabusing himself of the notion. "Are you sure you'll be okay in here by yourself tonight?"

Whitney nodded. "Yes, I'm sure. This hammock is great."

"Will you be warm enough? It gets kind of chilly in the evenings sometimes."

"Yes, I'll be fine."

Again, Theo looked as if he was about to say something. His eyes were studying her intently.

"What?"

He said nothing then suddenly reached up and drew his fingers slowly down the side of her cheek. His skin felt soft, despite the calluses on his fingertips. "Nothing. Stay safe, okay? If you have any trouble, just yell. I'll come running."

His blue eyes were mesmerizing, and had turned a dark sapphire color. Whitney was instantly lost in them. She was also so stunned by Theo's overture and her own reaction that she couldn't seem to speak. She resorted to nodding instead. Then, as quickly as it had begun, Theo withdrew his hand and turned.

"See you tomorrow. Sleep well," he called out over his shoulder.

Whitney watched him go, her hand touching her cheek where Theo's fingers had been only moments before. Her skin still tingled from his touch.

What was that all about? Did he have feelings for her, or was he just trying to make sure she felt safe and protected? Either way, what she couldn't figure out, was what, if anything, she wanted to do about it.

Theo walked as quickly as he could toward the beach. He was losing his mind. Yes, that was it. That was the only thing that could explain his bizarre behavior. He was a scientist. He operated on facts, and facts alone. He went over the facts as he walked, his feet stomping into the sand. Fact one: his wife and daughter had died in a horrible accident. Fact two:

he didn't want or need a new relationship. Opening up to a woman meant opening himself up to pain, which was unacceptable. Fact three: he felt so strongly about never falling in love again that he had moved to a deserted island to do his research and cut himself off almost completely from the civilized world. Fact four: he was not attracted to Whitney.

Or maybe he was…

The more time he spent with her, the more he was starting to learn about her, and there was an awful lot in that beautiful, spitfire package that he liked. He liked that she was tough as nails but touching a slimy frog made her scream. He liked that she said what she was thinking and didn't leave him guessing. He liked that she was straightforward and honest. He liked the way she hoarded fresh pineapple. He even liked the way her brows drew together and she looked at him with questions in her eyes as she tried to figure him out.

He stopped for a moment and gripped his hips with his hands, frustration eating away at him. Even if he admitted to himself that he liked her, and that was a big *if*, what was he prepared to do about it? The question gnawed at him and tied his stomach up in knots. As soon as they found help from a law-enforcement agency they could trust, this whole mess would be over and they would go back to their respective worlds.

So why did the thought of never seeing her again fill him with loneliness and foreboding?

TEN

A hand slipped over her mouth, silencing her and waking her from a deep sleep at the same time. Her body jolted and she started struggling against the other hand that was pushing her into the hammock. She glanced around frantically, but didn't have enough light to see who was touching her.

"Whitney? It's me, Theo." His voice came as a whisper. "Don't make a sound. The Coast Guard is here. They're searching for us. We need to disappear. Now."

She stopped struggling the moment she recognized his voice and rolled out of the hammock. Glancing around, she quickly gathered her bearings. It still seemed dark outside and she wondered fleetingly how long she had actually been asleep.

"What time is it?" she asked, even though her heart was beating frantically as the adrenaline spiked.

"A little after 5:00 a.m."

"Is the sun up enough for us to see?"

"Barely," Theo answered. "We'll just have to do the

best we can. We need to get to the kayak and get out of here as soon as we can before they come over here and start searching the area. Are you ready to go?"

She nodded, grabbed the backpack, pulled the gun out and stowed it in her waistband, then took one final look around to make sure she hadn't left anything behind. Finally, she slipped quietly out of the gazebo and they headed toward the dock where they had left the kayak the night before. Suddenly, she heard shouting coming from the direction of the bay. Whitney stopped and turned, torn. She didn't want to leave the two brothers at the mercy of a dirty captain in the Coast Guard, even if it meant that she and Theo would escape. She didn't know the captain, and didn't know what he was capable of.

"What about Mark and John?"

"They're causing a diversion, giving us a chance to get away," he whispered. "We heard the boat approaching. It woke us up. I was afraid it might have been the Coast Guard because the boat sounded rather large, so I explained that we couldn't let them find us because we were suspicious that they might have somehow been involved in your case. I didn't give them any details."

"Good call," she said approvingly. "The less they know, the better."

He nodded. "Before the boat got to the chickee, they told me to get to you and run. They said they'd give the newcomers a song and dance about the boat we'd left behind, but that won't slow the Coast Guard down for long. They'll probably be here to search that gazebo any minute. I don't think they'll hurt the two brothers, though, as long as they don't see any sign of us. They'll just ask them a lot of questions. In the meantime, we need to move."

"Okay," she agreed.

Theo took her hand and led her down an overgrown path into the mangroves. It had rained during the night and some of the ground was soupy and wet, but they were careful where they stepped. Theo used a stick and some brush and tried to erase any partial footprints left behind as they made their way to the dock.

Whitney didn't like running away from anyone, especially from a dirty law-enforcement officer, but these were desperate times, and desperate times called for desperate measures. She smiled to herself, remembering Jake Riley, her team leader in the Marshals' unit, teaching her patience in various situations over the last few years. It had been a hard lesson to learn, but one she had desperately needed. Jake's smooth Southern drawl mirrored his lifestyle. He was slow and deliberate, but extremely thorough and paid quite a bit of attention to detail. He often caught things that she missed with her headstrong and forceful attitude.

Her smile disappeared. Wasn't she running in her personal life, too? And unlike the situation with the drug dealers, in that context, it was a problem. After all, hadn't she come to the Keys just to avoid considering the news the doctor had given her just last week? She hadn't wanted to face the diagnosis or to admit that her life had been changed forever by a few short sentences the doctor had delivered after reviewing all of her latest tests. Funny how her future had changed so quickly from one of hopes and dreams to one of bitter disappointment in the space of just about five minutes.

Now wasn't the time for self-evaluation or recrimination, but she acknowledged that, sometime soon, she would have to sort through all of these feelings.

As they pushed the kayak into the water, Whitney jumped in the front seat and Theo took the seat in the back. He grabbed the paddle and immediately started steering the vessel toward the water trail that led deeper into the mangroves. It was hard to see, but he was doing an amazing job, and she was so thankful that he was sticking by her.

Suddenly they heard voices approaching and Theo quickly maneuvered the boat behind some brush and stopped paddling. There was no place to go. The water lapped quietly against the side of the kayak, but seemed to be booming in her ears, even though she was praying urgently that the men up on dry land couldn't hear it.

Dear God, please don't let them find us.

Whitney pulled out her weapon, prepared to defend them but unwilling to start the confrontation if a gun battle wasn't needed. She had agreed to working in a dangerous profession and the moment she had signed on the dotted line and become a US Marshal, she knew her life would sometimes be in peril.

But Theo was a scientist by trade. She did not want to put him in any more jeopardy or to risk his life if it wasn't necessary. The more she got to know him, the more she liked him. He had left the medical profession for some reason, yet he hadn't hesitated when his doctoring skills were needed to help someone in pain. Theo had also refused to abandon her, even when violent men with guns were chasing them and leaving her to her own devices would have been the easier path to take.

"If we find out you're lying, you'll be explaining yourself to the captain. He won't be as friendly as I've been, I can promise you that." The voice was deep and menacing, and it was one Whitney didn't recognize.

Mark answered, and she could hear the strain in his tone. "Look, I've already told you. We came back from setting up our snake traps, and the boat was tied to our chickee, just like it is now. We haven't even been on board to see if there's any paperwork in there that says who left it here. If it belongs to those people who reported it missing, like you said, then take it with our compliments. We just want to get back to work."

"You'll go back to work when I say you go back to work, do you understand?" The Coast Guard officer's voice was angry.

"Yeah, I get it. But I can't help you find someone

that is probably long gone from the area that I don't even know. We mind our own business here. We're only interested in doing our studies. You've seen our permits. We haven't done anything wrong."

The voices trailed off and they could tell Mark was leading the man to the small hut where Whitney had slept. They waited and, after about ten minutes, they heard the two men tromping back toward the chickee and the way they had come. Her heart continued to beat against her chest and her muscles were tense, ready to spring into action if needed.

Whitney and Theo waited a bit more, and finally heard two boat motors start up. The noise seemed deafening compared to the silence that had permeated the mangrove during the night, but eventually the motor noise seemed to dissipate and Whitney felt sure that the Coast Guard officers had gone, taking the drug dealers' boat with them. "I want to check and make sure John and Mark are okay. I'll be back." She kept her voice low, just in case she had misread the situation. "Can you get the kayak back to the dock?"

Theo nodded and maneuvered the small boat back where they'd started. Whitney jumped out and headed off down the trail, staying as quiet and inconspicuous as possible. It didn't take her long to get to the beach by the bay and she hid behind a stand of bushes and trees, trying to get a glimpse of the two scientists. She caught sight of them rather quickly.

They were repacking some of their boxes in the

chickee, and both were fine. She even heard Mark laugh at something John said. They seemed to be having a playful banter back and forth between them. Both the Coast Guard boat and the boat she and Theo had arrived in were nowhere to be seen.

A wave of relief flowed through Whitney and she said a silent prayer of thankfulness. John and Mark had helped them, and she was glad they were fine and had suffered no ill effects from the Coast Guard search party. She turned and hurried back to the dock where Theo was waiting, ready to navigate through the channels until they could find the help they needed to end this nightmare.

Theo didn't say a word when she returned, but his brow creased and there was a question in his eyes.

"They're fine," she reported quietly, still not wanting to make any more noise than necessary.

"Glad you checked," he responded, his voice equally low. He had tied the kayak next to the dock and was standing nearby, stretching his legs.

What little supplies they had were still in the backpack and already stowed in the middle section between the two seats. They had filled up their water bottles the night before with some of the water John had graciously shared, and Whitney reached for a bottle now and took a drink. Then she stretched a bit, as well, trying to get the tightness out of her muscles that the adrenaline was causing. A moment later she got into the front of the kayak and Theo followed suit, settling in the seat in the rear. He glanced at the markers and started paddling, heading into the twists and turns of the mangrove trail.

A couple of hours later Theo was still carefully guiding the kayak down the creek. The small waterway was lined on both sides with a web of mangrove branches and leaves, and the watercourse widened and shrank as they traveled, changing slowly as they went deeper into the park to having more and more solid land around them.

They only had one paddle, so he had promised to take turns and let Whitney paddle some later, but for now, he found himself relishing the quiet as the Everglades came alive with the morning light. Birds were chirping, and cicadas and crickets were singing. And while he knew danger was only a short distance away, he couldn't keep himself from enjoying the environment around him. He glanced at the water and saw fish both big and small darting from under the kayak as his strokes sliced the water.

Thoughts of his daughter came unbidden to his mind. She would have loved to see these fish. For her fifth birthday, she had insisted that all she'd wanted was a goldfish, and her wish had been granted. They had already replaced the poor creature twice because his little girl kept overfeeding it, despite the many lessons they had given her in how to take care of the fish. It was all because of that movie they had downloaded that had the little clownfish. After seeing that, all his daughter had talked about was fish and the ocean. And how, when she grew up, she was going to work on a boat so she could see fish all day. His wife had even gotten her a new comforter and pillow set imprinted with several clownfish playfully darting around the sea anemones on the ocean floor.

Theo smiled at the memories, lost in thought. They had been planning a trip to the aquarium in Atlanta, but had never made it. Not before that awful day that had robbed him of his precious little girl forever...

"This place is like a giant maze. Are you sure we're going the right way? There's another marker, but it's green instead of red like the last few."

Whitney's words brought him into the here and now. He suddenly realized he had been paddling in silence for quite a while, lost in his memories. They had been bittersweet, and left his heart tight with pain. He had lost so much...

He tried to push the thoughts aside. He could not change the past and, if he wasn't careful, he wouldn't have much of a future, either. He glanced over at the marker she was pointing at. "No, I'm not sure. I don't know why that one is a different color, but I didn't see another way to turn, so it seems like we should keep going forward."

Whitney shrugged. "That makes sense. I sure wish John or Mark had given us a map, but I doubt they even had one with them. I don't think they even use one anymore." She glanced at the sky. "I think a storm really is coming, despite the models the brothers were talking about that showed it going out into the Atlantic. It rained last night, but the air is still heavy, and the wind is picking up. I think more rain is on the way."

"You're probably right," Theo agreed. He'd noticed the sky himself and was starting to worry. Dark clouds were on the horizon and heading right for them, and a definite breeze was starting to pick up from the south, just as Whitney had noticed. They hadn't passed a single building yet or anything resembling a ranger station, and Theo was hoping he hadn't accidentally gotten them lost somehow.

That made him nervous because there was no place to take refuge if a storm came upon them. And even if they did find shelter, they didn't have the luxury of waiting somewhere for a few days until the weather improved. They had to keep pushing into the park until they found help. The Coast Guard team had already found their boat, and it was fairly obvious which direction Whitney and Theo must have gone to escape. If the Coast Guard captain was dirty, as they suspected, he no doubt would report his findings to the drug dealers, who would quickly have the park exits blocked, if they didn't already have them covered. Theo felt like a giant net was closing in around him.

He had no illusions about what would happen to them if they were discovered. The drug dealers would kill them both. Whitney had seen too much, and they wouldn't know what she had told Theo. They would take him out, too, just to cover their tracks.

Theo tried to focus on the positive aspects of the trip, and watch Whitney as she energetically took in the scenery around her. She had turned to face him several times so they could talk now and then, and her features had filled with wonder and delight as she'd noticed the birds, flowers and foliage of the Everglades. That same delight had quickly turned to revulsion and fear at the sight of several alligators and one snake that they had passed on their journey. He had repeatedly assured her that they were safe in the kayak, and she seemed to believe him, for the most part.

Theo enjoyed watching her reactions. Whitney was a wonder, and he was still trying to figure her out as she continued to surprise him. He had never been around a person that was so vivacious, and her vibrant personality was like a tonic, slowly healing him from his past. His wife had been a wonderful lady, and he'd loved her deeply, but her introverted personality had been reserved and quiet, much like his own. Whitney was the opposite and, although he hadn't sought her out, he had to admit, he was enjoying their time together, despite the trepidation that kept creeping up his spine whenever he thought about who was chasing them and why.

Would they survive this ordeal? At this point, Theo wasn't even sure they would make it through the day, but he had to admit, he felt more alive than he had in months.

He was so deep in contemplation that he didn't even hear the canoe approaching them from behind.

ELEVEN

The first bullet hit the front of the kayak, mere inches from where Whitney was sitting. She pulled her weapon and instantly turned, seeking the shooter. The sound of the shot was still echoing across the marsh grasses when the second shot was fired, and she ducked instinctively, leaning as close to the kayak's top as she could, her weapon still out and pointing toward the source. The only problem was, she couldn't see who was firing at them.

The kayak shimmied in the water as Theo also leaned close to the boat, but there was really no place for either of them to go.

"Put your hands up!" a deep voice ordered. "Now!"

A seed of dread started growing in Whitney's stomach. She didn't need to see the villain to know who was after them. She recognized that voice. It was the same deep voice of Lopez's short companion—the guy who had tried to shoot her on the tour boat when this whole adventure had started.

She and Theo both slowly raised their hands and

their eyes met. Whitney tried to instill hope in her expression, but their situation suddenly seemed very bleak. She was still holding her gun and Theo still grasped the paddle in one of his raised fists. But there was really nothing they could do to defend themselves against this latest threat, even with those weapons available to them.

If she took a chance and fired her weapon now, it was likely that Theo would get shot in the cross fire, so using the gun wasn't really a viable option. Adrenaline started pumping through Whitney's veins and she kept herself alert, waiting for a chance to act. Were the drug dealers going to kill them right here and now, leaving their bodies for alligator bait? The thought was a chilling one and she immediately started praying as she stretched to get a better view of the pursuers.

It was hard to see the men that were approaching them because of the angle of their kayak in the water. To make matters worse, the sun had disappeared and given way to rain a short time ago, and the misty weather further obstructed her view. The rain started coming down a little stronger, and their kayak turned a bit since Theo had quit paddling.

The canoe that was following them suddenly came into view and, just as Whitney had dreaded, she saw the short man with the deep voice in the front seat of the boat about forty feet behind them. To her dismay, Jose, the man she had tied up on Theo's island, sat in the back of the boat and was paddling, despite a bandage tied around his upper arm from where she had shot him. The man she'd dubbed "Shorty" was holding an automatic pistol at them. It was hard to tell, but Whitney thought it looked like a .45—a very lethal gun that had a lot of power.

"Don't move an eyelash," Shorty commanded as the canoe came forward and eventually knocked against the hull of the kayak.

She considered fighting them—canoes tipped over pretty easily, didn't they? The only problem was, she was deathly afraid of going into the water herself, and didn't want to take a chance of sporting an alligator bite like John's on her own arm. She noticed that Theo seemed to be considering a fight, as well—after all, he still had the paddle in his hand. Their eyes met and she shook her head, almost imperceptibly. He got the message and relaxed his arm.

Whitney hoped she wasn't making a giant mistake by allowing the drug dealers to get so close to them, but she had decided to just wait and bide her time for a better opportunity to escape. She trusted her instincts, but gritted her teeth in frustration and fisted her hand, hating the helpless feelings that were rolling over her.

The canoe got close enough that Shorty was able to reach over to the kayak, and once he did so, he yanked the gun out of Whitney's hand. "You've led us on quite a chase, but it's over now. I hope you enjoyed your little boat ride, because it was the last one you'll ever get to take."

He motioned with her gun at Theo. "Keep paddling, buddy. Go straight ahead. I want to get out of this rain, and there's an empty ranger station about a half mile ahead. Just follow this waterway. And remember, we're right behind you and I've got my weapon pointed right at your pretty little girlfriend if you make any sudden moves."

Whitney raised an eyebrow. Again with the girlfriend comments? She glanced up at Theo and noticed he had a small, almost imperceptible smile on his face, as if he could read her thoughts. Despite everything that was happening to them, he could still find something to smile about. She liked that about him. She brushed the rain off her face and turned back to the front of the kayak as Theo slowly put the paddle in the water and started pushing them forward.

Thunder suddenly boomed above and Shorty's deep voice sounded behind them. "This is no pleasure cruise. Put some muscle into it and let's get out of this rain!"

Theo didn't have a plan. He glanced up at Whitney as he bent forward and really pulled the paddle through the water. He hoped she had figured some way out of this mess. Her back was straight, and with the rain plastering her clothes against her skin, it was easy to see that her muscles were tight and ready to spring into action. He knew she was like a powder keg inside, despite her calm and nonthreatening exterior. She was well trained, and he knew she saw things that he would miss even on his best day—things they could use to their advantage if just given half a chance.

It was interesting that he was learning to read her so well—even though they had only known each other for a couple of days. He didn't know how she would get them out of this one, or if it was even possible for them to break away from this newest threat, but he kept his eyes and ears open, looking for any chance to help Whitney, just in case she saw an opportunity for them to escape.

He continued to paddle as the storm rolled in. What had begun as a misty rain was now a regular downpour, and it was raining so hard it was difficult to even see straight. Large drops of water pelted against them and there was nothing to block them from the weather assault that had tripled in strength in a matter of minutes. The wind had picked up, as well, and Theo found himself paddling into the gusts, making it even harder to make any progress. He glanced behind him at the drug dealers, and noticed that they were also struggling against the elements. As he watched, Jose lost his hat to the wind and it went flying into the water, several yards behind them.

Theo smiled and turned back, still paddling toward the building the short guy had mentioned. He couldn't see it yet, especially since his glasses were covered with rain water, but he imagined they would come upon it soon and it would give them some shelter from this storm.

About fifteen minutes later they arrived on a beach of sorts. It was small—only about twenty feet long—but there was a gradual incline of sand rather than mangrove roots or marshland, and the land was actually solid and walkable, even though the water was steadily rising as they landed their boats and disembarked. In the distance, Theo could just make out a small ranger station and a dock that bordered the water.

"Pull the boats out and bring them with us," Shorty ordered, his gun still wavering between Theo and Whitney.

"Are you going to help?" Jose whined. "These boats are heavy." He was obviously not enjoying the sudden storm and was anxious to get out of the rain. Despite his size, the expression on his face made him appear like a petulant child.

Some plant fronds blew toward them and caught against Whitney's legs. She sidestepped them, but the motion made Shorty nervous.

"My job is to hold the gun. Your job is to get those boats on higher ground. Do it, and do it now." Shorty motioned with the weapon, his patience clearly ebbing, as well.

There was only one way to quickly get out of the storm. Whitney grabbed the front of their kayak while Theo took hold of the back. Jose clutched the front of the canoe and followed them toward the building, dragging the canoe behind him. Luckily for him, the drug dealers' boat was only about fourteen feet long, and on the smallish side for a canoe, so one person could manage it fairly well.

Theo did his best to ignore Jose and focus instead on doing as much as he could to help Whitney with their kayak. Although it wasn't very heavy, it was rather awkward to maneuver, especially with the wind gusting against the thermoformed plastic. Still, they were able to get the boats up to the outside of the building and wedge them both between two trees to keep the wind from destroying them. Theo then reached over and grabbed their backpack, which Shorty immediately took from him and searched. Finding nothing of interest inside, he tossed it on the ground at Theo's feet. "Let's go."

Theo leaned over, grabbed the backpack and slung it over his shoulder, very aware that Shorty was keeping the gun trained on them the entire time.

He followed them up to the front porch, where they got their first reprieve from some of the rain, and then started entering the code on the lock that secured the door. It opened with a click, and Shorty pointed them inside the building, then followed them in and closed the door firmly behind him. He motioned with his weapon toward Jose. "Go ahead and zip them up."

Theo wasn't sure what the lingo meant, but he stood in front of Whitney, offering her what little protection he could. He was realistic, however. There wasn't anything he could do against the gun, and since the drug dealer had taken the weapon Whitney had been carrying, they were basically defenseless. And, for all he knew, Jose had a gun, as well, tucked away somewhere on his person. A wave of adrenaline surged through Theo and he turned and met Whitney's eyes. Should they attack, despite the guns, and run for their freedom?

But where would they go? As Whitney shook her head in response to his silent question, disappointment swamped him, even though he knew she was right. Now wasn't the time. The storm had pinned them down, and running around lost in the Everglades during a gale held no appeal. They would watch and wait for a better opportunity. But would they get one?

Jose pulled several colored zip ties out of his pocket. "Give me your hands," he ordered gruffly, motioning to Theo.

Theo held out his arms, as if he was getting handcuffed, and the man pulled against the plastic strip and secured his wrists. Jose then physically pushed him out of the way and turned to Whitney, whose eyes were alert and vigilant. Jose zip-tied her hands, and then Shorty pushed the two trussed victims farther into the small room.

The building had one main room that contained a counter, and behind it, three desks and office chairs, as well as a bathroom and a supply room. Each desk had an assortment of papers strewed around, as if the workers would be returning at any moment. Theo could just make out a smaller office through an open door at the back, but it was hard to see inside or to tell what the room might contain. Despite the condition of the office, he was fairly certain the building hadn't been recently utilized. A layer of dust covered everything within sight, and there were large spiderwebs in two of the four corners.

Shorty pushed them toward the supply room, kicked the door open wider than it had been, and motioned for them to go inside. "After you," he said with a sneer.

Theo and Whitney moved into the room and Shorty closed and locked the door behind them. Theo sighed as he glanced around. There wasn't much to the supply room beyond a couple of shelving units and a copy machine. There was a small window that let in some light, but it was too small to crawl through. There wasn't any furniture, and he didn't see any food or useful items that would help their escape. One of the shelves contained mostly office supplies, such as pencils, pens, and paper for the copy machine, while the other contained boxes of T-shirts and hats that the rangers sold in the gift shop at the park entrance.

"Do you see any scissors?" Theo asked. He kept his voice low, realizing that the men outside could probably hear them if they spoke too loudly.

Whitney was checking through the boxes and looking around, as well, despite being hampered by the zip tie. "Nothing so far," she responded, also keeping her tone low. "Nothing sharp enough to cut through plastic." She checked a few more boxes, then turned. "Guess we'll have to get out of these the old-fashioned way."

Theo's eyebrow quirked. "The old-fashioned way?"

Whitney smiled, as if she knew a special secret, and gave him a wink, as well. She had a nice smile. He thought back, trying to remember if she had smiled at him like that before. It made her appear as if she was up to something, not trussed up like a Thanksgiving turkey.

Of course, there had been very little to smile about over the last couple of days, and he didn't know all of her looks and expressions. Still, despite her usual positive attitude, at times, she seemed to have a tinge of sadness about her. He couldn't really put his finger on what made him think so—she'd certainly never claimed to be anything but a tourist on vacation. But something about her general demeanor made him think there was definitely something going on under the surface that worried her. He wondered if they would get close enough during this ordeal to actually talk and share any truly personal details about themselves, or if she would even feel comfortable confiding her intimate thoughts to him.

That thought left him pondering for a moment. Did he want to tell Whitney about his wife and daughter's death? Theo had always been a very private person. He rarely opened up to others. Yet, even so, there was something about Whitney that drew him to her—something that made him want to protect her and bare his soul to her. Some vulnerability seemed to exist that she might not even recognize in herself.

Was he totally misreading her?

It was certainly possible. He was no expert in the female species. But Whitney challenged him to think about something other than himself and his experiments, and he found himself actually enjoying the quandary that this beautiful woman presented.

He found her utterly fascinating.

Theo watched as she grabbed the end of the zip tie with her teeth and maneuvered it so the locking mechanism was right in the middle between her hands. Then she pulled the tie even tighter against her skin.

"Are you tightening that?" he asked incredulously.

"Yep," she responded with a wink. She raised her bound hands above her head, then brought them down quickly into her stomach. Her elbows flared out and it looked as if she was trying to have her shoulder blades touch. There was a short snap, and the zip tie broke, right by the locking mechanism, freeing her hands.

Theo was amazed. He didn't know it was possible to escape zip ties, but Whitney had just made it look incredibly easy. He followed her example, and was soon free himself, rubbing his wrists where the tie had been biting into his skin only moments before.

"If they want to zip-tie us again, put your hands like you did before—like you're about to get handcuffed with your fists clenched, your palms down and your thumbs together. Then, unclench your hands and turn them so your thumbs are up." She demonstrated with her own hands, then grabbed his hands, and showed him what she was talking about. "Yeah, that's right. Then just start working your hands out, starting with your thumbs. It takes a little bit of work, but you can do it, and it doesn't hurt quite as much as breaking the tie like we just did."

It made sense. He smiled in appreciation. "How did you ever learn this?"

Shrugging, she met his eye, "A few years ago, bad guys started using zip ties to restrain victims in home invasions and robberies, so we were trained on how to break free if the need ever arose. Then, of course, being the competitive group we are, we had to try to see who could escape the fastest. We even had team contests during an ice-breaker at a training program once. It was actually a lot of fun."

Theo shook his head. "Well, I'm sure glad you did. You made short work of those." He pulled off his glasses and wiped them on his T-shirt. Finally he could see again. "I'm getting hungry. Want a power bar?"

Whitney nodded. "Sure thing, unless you have some fried chicken in there. I could eat a few pieces right about now."

"Yes," Theo added, "with coleslaw, potato salad and a large glass of sweet tea."

"Don't forget the biscuits and butter," Whitney quipped. "Or maybe a bit of strawberry jam."

He pulled out the power bar. "But until we can get a good Southern meal, this will have to do."

Theo handed her a bar. She took it and opened it, then bit off a large chunk. He liked the way she ate with enthusiasm, as if she was savoring every bite. She seemed to do everything with gusto. It was a very endearing personality trait.

She walked over to the door and tried the knob, then turned and shrugged at him. Neither of them was surprised that it was locked. She put her ear up against the crack then suddenly froze.

"What do you hear?" Theo asked, trying to keep the anxiousness out of his voice.

Whitney held up her finger to silence him, then took another bite of the power bar but kept her ear pressed against the wood.

"They're arguing," she whispered. "Jose is saying they should just shoot us and leave us in the swamp." She grinned. "I guess he still hasn't forgiven me for tying him up and shooting him on your island." She paused with a raised finger. "Now he's saying he's afraid of the weather and doesn't want to get stuck here for the next few days. He thinks it is a hurricane, not just a bad storm." She took another bite of the power bar. "He says if they throw our bodies in the water, the alligators will get us and no one will ever even miss us."

Theo shook his head. He couldn't keep the anxiety from creeping inside him, no matter how hard he tried. He fisted his hands, then said a short but heartfelt prayer. *God, please help us find a way out of this mess.*

TWELVE

The men were no longer talking. Now they were shouting at each other. Whitney pressed her ear against the crack between the door and the frame again, then turned and reported what she'd heard to Theo. "I'm not sure I'm catching everything because now they're yelling in Spanish and English. My Spanish is not so great. The short guy is pretty angry. He's saying something about waiting to hear from El Jefe. I've heard that name before. He says this whole thing has blown up into one giant mess, and he can't do anything to us without El Jefe's approval. I think this El Jefe guy has to be the one pulling all of the strings with the drug cartel."

She paused again and took another bite, chewing thoughtfully as she listened at the door. "Jose is threatening to kill us all and just disappear…" She glanced back at Theo. "Now the short one is saying that they figured out I am a US Marshal, and El Jefe needs to know that before they make any other moves." She leaned back. "That's unfortunate. I was hoping they wouldn't figure that out."

Theo seemed surprised. "Why?"

"Because they don't guard me as closely if they think I'm just a helpless tourist. I use that to my advantage whenever I can." She pulled away from the door just as it rattled and shook. There was a large thumping sound, as if the two men had begun physically fighting and the battle suddenly brought them up against the door. She motioned to Theo. "Step back, just in case. They both have guns and might end up shooting each other."

Whitney didn't know quite what to expect, but she did know she didn't want Theo hurt if the scuffle escalated any further. She started pulling against the wooden shelving unit, trying to push it in front of the door to add one more buffer between them and a bullet if the fight in the other room became lethal. Theo started helping her and together they moved it in front of the door. It was full of office supplies, including paper and notebooks, so Whitney hoped that if a gun did go off, they would be somewhat protected. She motioned to the copy machine and they moved it to the center of the room, as well, then crouched behind it.

They hovered there together as the fight in the other room intensified. The argument was now completely yelled in Spanish alone. Even though Whitney's Spanish was rusty, the intent was clear. The short man wanted to get permission before acting.

José wanted to save himself and get somewhere safe before the storm got any worse.

Suddenly there was a gunshot and the sound echoed across the room. Whitney tensed, but the bullet must have gone in a different direction because she didn't see any evidence that it had entered the storage room where they were being held. Silence followed; the only thing they could hear was the wind blowing outside and gusting against the building. Then they heard a door slam. Had one of the men just left the building? It was time to take a chance and find out.

She motioned for Theo to continue to stay out of the way, then moved the shelving unit aside and gave the door a vicious kick. It shuddered against the frame. What she wouldn't give for a good pair of boots! All she had on her feet were the clogs Theo had given her back on the island. They were made from soft rubber—hardly the material needed to break down doors. Still, she had to keep trying. She kicked the door again and felt the wood start to buckle. A third kick put a large hole in the hollow door near the doorknob.

Whitney reached up through the hole, unlocked the knob and the dead bolt, then slowly opened the door, unsure of what she would find. Was José waiting for her around the corner, waiting to pay her back for disarming him at Theo's house? Her heart was beating a mile a minute. The front door to the building was swinging on the hinges and being tossed to and fro by the wind. Whitney quickly crossed the room and closed the door, stopping the racket and also keeping the rain out that had started pouring in through the opening.

She turned quickly and scanned the room. Theo had emerged and was standing over Shorty, who was slumped against the front cabin wall. A bullet hole was visible on his chest, a red circle of blood pooling on his shirt. Theo pulled his hand away from the man's neck, then closed the man's eyes, which were staring sightlessly across the room. "No pulse. He's gone."

Whitney nodded. "Can you get his gun and phone?"

Theo ran his hands over Shorty's pockets. "Looks like both are gone. I imagine Jose grabbed both on his way out of the building."

Whitney sighed and rolled her eyes. "Good grief, we just can't catch a break." She shook her head. "Does he have anything that will help us?"

Theo searched the rest of the man's belongings, then shrugged. "Doesn't look like it. He doesn't even have any ID or a wallet in his pocket."

She quickly searched the rest of the building. The bathroom was empty, as well as the small office at the back. There was really no place to hide. "The building is clear. Jose must have disappeared right after he pulled the trigger. He's got to know Shorty was pretty high up in the cartel food chain. I'm sure his life isn't worth beans now. Once El Jefe figures out what happened, I bet the next contract he orders will be for Jose's life."

She looked out through the window and watched

the storm blow and bend the trees. The weather was getting worse. Branches and debris were already strewed around the building, and plants were bending and breaking in the wind. She'd been through enough tropical storms and hurricanes during her life in Florida to know a dangerous storm when she saw one. The rain had let up a bit, but she knew it would be back with a vengeance in only a few minutes. "That guy probably grabbed the canoe and is going to try to head out to find higher ground. That seems like a pretty dumb move, though. He's not going to get far in this storm."

"I think so, too," Theo concurred. "If it's all the same to you, I believe we should stay here for the time being. Those winds are pretty strong out there. It's not safe to be in the kayak, and I don't see any other mode of transportation available."

"I agree." She nodded. "Let's do a search and see if we can find a radio or other way to call for help." She winked at him. "Finding a stash of food would be okay, too. That meal yesterday with John and Mark spoiled me."

"No kidding. That fish was amazing. Power bars just aren't the same."

They spent the next half an hour going through each drawer and shelf in the small building. Unfortunately, they didn't find anything that would be useful for communicating with the outside world.

There was a small sink and coffee station in the small office in the back, and Whitney made them both a cup of coffee in case they lost power due to the storm and couldn't make some later. She kept looking around, relief flooding through her when she found a microwave and four cans of soup in a cabinet above it, as well as a liberal supply of paper goods. She wasn't hungry now since she'd just snacked on the power bar, but it was nice to know they would have something for later since it didn't look like they were going anywhere anytime soon.

The storm continued to build outside, the wind and rain pelting the building. They heard a loud crash and rushed to the window to get a glimpse of what had caused the noise. A large pine tree behind the building had come down, but had thankfully missed the building.

Whitney crossed her arms and rubbed her shoulders. She wished the windows had shutters, so she could at least protect them from flying debris if something blew against the glass and broke through. She didn't like storms, and really didn't like being in this small ranger station with one raging outside. Whenever a hurricane looked like it was going to hit Tallahassee, she'd packed up and fled to Atlanta, or to one of her brothers' houses.

She glanced around the room and her eyes landed on Shorty. The dead body on the floor didn't bother her. The idea that a hurricane was blowing outside while she was stuck in this rickety old building, however, made her very nervous.

Theo must have noticed. He motioned for her to

follow him into the center of the room by the interior wall and then sank to the floor, using the wall as back support.

Whitney took one last look around, then followed and sat next to him, her coffee cup still in her hand. He had probably picked the safest place in the building to go. Experts usually recommended hiding in an interior bathroom or closet if a person was stuck in a home during a hurricane; those were the most structurally safe locations. Of course, if the hurricane became a category 4 or 5, there would be nothing left after a storm, regardless of where they hid. Without some sort of radio or internet access, however, there was nothing else that she and Theo could really do to prepare.

She said a silent prayer, asking God to protect them from the violent storm.

Theo was again noticing little details about Whitney. He knew she didn't like frogs or alligators, but apparently he could also add storms to the list. She had been pacing before, her arms and hands constantly in motion, as if she just couldn't keep still. He took her hand and leaned back, closing his eyes, hoping that she would find the contact comforting and also less objectionable if he wasn't looking at her when he touched her.

She allowed the contact once again, and he was pleasantly surprised that she didn't pull away. They sat in silence for several minutes, just listening to the storm raging outside. He'd meant to comfort her with his actions, but he found himself enjoying the contact more than he wanted to admit. Her skin was soft like satin, and just knowing she was nearby and facing these obstacles with him soothed the anxiety in his own heart.

"So tell me the story of your life," Theo said quietly, still not looking at her.

Whitney gave a small laugh. "Wow, you must really be bored."

He opened his eyes and found that she was looking at him intently. He grinned. "Not at all. I'd just like to get to know you better."

"There's not much to tell," she answered with a shrug. "But truth be told, I'd rather hear about you."

"Nice deflection," he noted. "I don't usually talk about myself."

She smiled. "Yeah, I guessed that. But I've told you about my brothers and why I went into law enforcement. I think it's your turn to share a little."

He pressed his lips into a thin line. She had a point, yet opening up to her still made him uneasy, despite the fact that she was growing on him. He drew his thumb across the back of her hand, trying to decide if he was ready to talk about his past or not. It was a tough decision. He was a very private person, and his introverted personality had driven him even further into solitude after he had gone through his family's tragedy. Was he ready to reach out to this woman and open himself up for pain once again?

Even if friendship was all that they ever shared, he still didn't know if he could stand losing someone again, and in their current situation, losing her was a definite possibility.

She must have sensed his hesitation and taken pity on him. Her next words confirmed it. "Tell you what—let's make a deal." She squeezed his hand but didn't break the contact. "I'll ask you three questions. Then, in return, I'll let you ask me three. If you survive the first round, we might do another, but if three questions are all you want to answer, we'll stop there. What do you think?"

He tilted his head to the side, considering her words. "Law-enforcement officers are probably pros at digging answers out of people. Are you sure you can stop at three questions?"

She put her hand over her heart. "I promise. Only three, unless you agree to answer another three after you've had your turn." She nudged him playfully. "I've had CPR training. If the shock of talking about yourself causes your heart to stop, I promise, I know how to get it beating again."

He laughed outright. "Oh really?" Still, he had to admit, he was enjoying her banter, and the entire conversation was keeping their minds off the storm, the dead body across the room and the drug dealers breathing down their necks.

"Okay," he finally agreed. "Take your best shot."

She beamed as if he'd just given her a precious gift and tapped her cheek as if she needed all the help she could get with choosing her questions carefully. "If I only get three, I need to make sure they count."

Despite the fact that he had agreed to this game, he could feel a tightness in his chest as he worried about what she was going to ask. He was uncomfortable with baring his soul. Why had he decided to play this game? Hopefully she would stick to impersonal, generic questions.

"Ready?" She gave him a side-eyed glance.

"Sure. Go for it."

"Okay. Question number one. How old are you?"

He blinked. "What?"

Whitney shrugged. "I'm guessing you're in your thirties, but I'm not very good at knowing ages on sight, so I admit, I could be way off in my estimation. You might be almost fifty."

He raised an eyebrow, then saw the mirth in her eyes shimmering just below the surface. "So I look fifty to you?"

She shrugged. "It's a definite possibility. You might be closer to sixty. I think I saw some AARP magazines at your house on the coffee table, and wasn't there a walker stored in your bedroom closet?" She sighed dramatically. "Don't worry. At least you're aging gracefully. You still look pretty good for a man with your advanced years."

Tension drained from Theo as he laughed at the funny expression on her face. He had to give her points for putting him at ease. He could tell she had deliberately asked something simple and made a joke out of it to help him feel comfortable. "You're pretty good at this game. I'm thirty-six. My birthday is in March. Next?"

"Okay. Question number two." She tapped her cheek again with her finger. "Do you believe in God?"

Theo nodded. Although he had fallen away from his faith after his wife and daughter had died, it was still a part of him, and he would never deny God's existence. "I do. I'm a Christian. My faith is very important to me, even though I've stumbled with it lately. I do miss attending church, though, since I've been living on the island. Next?"

Whitney squeezed his hand again. "Okay. Good. I'm glad you said that. Last question." She leaned forward so their eyes met. "Why are you so sad?"

His heart was suddenly thumping against his chest and it was all he could do to maintain eye contact. He swallowed. "Do I seem sad to you?"

She nodded. "Very. I realize I haven't known you very long, but it's like someone turned a light off inside you. I've been wondering why ever since I met you."

Theo looked away. For a moment or two, he was lost in memories. Finally he returned his gaze to Whitney's face. "Four years ago, I had everything I ever wanted in life. I was a doctor in the emergency room up in Tampa and my career was flourishing. I was married to a beautiful woman and I had a sweet five-year-old daughter."

"And then?"

"I lost everything in one afternoon. My wife was driving my daughter to ballet class and she was hit head-on by a teenage driver who was texting his girl-friend from behind the wheel. They brought them to the ER where I was working, but I wasn't able to save them. I lost them both."

He finally released her hand so he could take off his glasses and wipe his eyes where tears had begun to make his vision swim.

"Theo, I'm so sorry." Whitney cupped his cheek with her hand for a moment then leaned back. "I'm sure you did your best."

"I did, but it wasn't enough. I tried to pull in a surgeon or even another doctor to help, but there had been two other accidents that occurred at about the same time, and all of the victims from each of the accidents seemed to arrive at the same time. It was a nightmare." He put his hand over hers before she could move it, then twined their fingers. "After that, I just couldn't practice medicine anymore. If I couldn't even help my own family, what good was I as a doctor?"

Whitney shook her head. "That's not fair. I'm sure you've helped hundreds of people with your medical skills. That talent is a gift from God."

He shrugged. "A short time later, a friend of mine who was good at grant writing helped me apply for the coral project grant. I got the award, and started working from the island. I had an undergraduate dual degree in biology and environmental science, and did some research work before I went to medical school, so they thought I would be the perfect candidate." He blew out a breath. "So far, they seemed pleased with the results and even increased my funding, but there is still a lot of work to be done."

"Slacker." She smiled, teasing him with her words and her expression. "Only two undergraduate degrees? Most people I know have three or four."

He made a face himself. "Oh really?"

"Yes, really." She laughed out loud this time and the tone was like music to his ears.

She could have kept pressing for details about his wife and daughter's deaths, but instead, she was gently guiding the conversation into safer territory, letting him decide how much to share. He appreciated her sensitivity. "You must hang out with some pretty brainy people."

She winked at him. "They don't let just *anybody* become a US Marshal, you know."

"I'm starting to realize that." This time he squeezed her fingers. "Okay. My turn."

She rolled her shoulders as if preparing for the ultimate challenge. "Okay, Mr. Brilliant. Lay it on me. I'm ready."

"Okay. Question number one. How old are you?"

She laughed again. "Lofting softballs at me, are you? Toughening me up for the fast pitch?"

He shrugged. "It's a serious question. I'm even worse at guessing a person's age than you are."

"Give me your best guess."

"No way. I learned my lesson a long time ago. A man can never guess a woman's age, or her weight. Not if he wants to survive."

Whitney shook her head. "Oh please." Her tone was playful. "Okay, you win. I just turned thirty last month."

"Ah, that's exactly what I was going to guess."

"You were not!" she protested, laughter in her eyes.

"Question number two—"

Suddenly a frantic knock sounded at the door. Theo had been so involved in their repartee that he had momentarily forgotten their desperate situation. The reality came crashing back down around him as he stood and headed for the door. He motioned to Whitney. "Let me do this. Stay out of sight."

There was no way to look out the door to see who was banging on it. He took a deep breath, then unlocked the dead bolt, fully expecting a gun barrel to be shoved in his face. Had the drug dealers tracked them down in the middle of a hurricane? They were just that tenacious. Anything was possible. His pulse sped up as he turned the knob and threw open the door.

THIRTEEN

"Please help us!"

Whitney approached the door at the sound of the plea for help. She stopped next to Theo, who still had a look of surprise on his face. There was no drug dealer with a gun at the door. Instead there was a Hispanic couple with three children of various ages clinging to them. They were all soaking wet, wind-blown and looked as if they were about to fall down.

"Come in, come in!" She motioned as the wind whipped around them on the porch.

"Our b-boat sank," the man sputtered as Theo grabbed him as he started falling to the ground. "It was all we could do to make it here in one piece."

Whitney reached for a little girl that seemed about four years old. She was shivering, but Whitney guessed it was more from fear than the cold since the weather was still rather warm despite the storm. She hugged her close and drew her into the room. The girl came willingly, as if she needed the warmth of Whitney's arms to feel safe.

The mom gave Whitney an appreciative glance. "Thanks. I wish I could grow another pair of arms." The other two children, a boy and girl that seemed about eight or so, were wrapped around her and making it hard for her to even walk. She ushered them in behind Theo and her husband, and Whitney stood, still holding the girl, and closed the door firmly behind them.

Whitney shared a look with Theo. He nodded and they moved the new arrivals into the small office, away from Shorty's body. She didn't want the children scared by the corpse lying on the floor in a pool of blood. Apparently, Theo had understood her apprehension and agreed with her. Although Whitney didn't like the idea of messing with a crime scene before the authorities could process the evidence, there was no way she was going to leave that man's body in plain sight where it would traumatize the kids. As soon as they got a chance, they would have to do something about that.

The kids...

Right before she had left Tallahassee, the doctor had given her the fateful news. *You will never have children.* She could still hear the doctor's voice, echoing in her head with the finality of the statement being emphasized over and over in her brain. *You will never have children.*

She had always wanted a family, and the news had been so devastating that she'd had to leave town to get away from everything that reminded her of her broken dreams. Even being around children now made her heart hurt, and the little girl in her arms was no exception. Every toothless grin, every toy aisle in every store and every sticky-fingered child reminded her that she was a failure.

I can never have children. Ever.

And now she had a four-year-old hanging on to her neck for dear life. Whitney's heart was beating a mile a minute in trepidation. The girl felt so heavy and right in her arms. What she wouldn't give for a child of her own! But she would never have that. It was a bitter pill to swallow. Still, she couldn't let the child just cling there, wet, ragged and traumatized, seeking comfort that she was willing to receive even from a complete and total stranger. The girl's mother obviously had her hands full, and was exhausted herself. This little one needed help, and Whitney was available and willing.

She hugged the child to her, then pulled back to get a better look at her face so she could reassure her. The girl had somehow managed to put her thumb in her mouth, and Whitney recognized the almond-shaped eyes and other facial features of a child with Down syndrome. "Our boat sank," the girl said simply.

"I'm so sorry," Whitney said, pulling her close again as she sat in a chair. "You're safe now. I promise." She started rocking the child gently back and forth, and the girl relaxed against her. Whitney brushed the long dark hair out of her eyes. "What's your name?" she asked gently.

"I'm Melissa." The girl had taken her thumb out of her mouth long enough to respond then quickly slid it back in again.

"We're the Martinezes," the man volunteered from a seated position by the wall where Theo had been sitting only moments before. "I'm David, and this is my wife, Geri." His wife had settled in next to him on the floor, taking the other two children with her.

"These two are Analena and Carlos." The kids looked up but didn't speak. Geri hugged them affectionately. "They're both a little shy and probably won't say much until they warm up to you. Please don't take it personally."

"Not a problem," Whitney answered, still hugging Melissa. "We've had a rough day today, too, but it sounds like yours was even worse."

"The storm wasn't supposed to even come in this direction," David noted. "We checked the news a couple of days ago when we first set out on this camping trip. It was just a tropical storm then, and it wasn't even supposed to hit the USA. The weatherman said it was just going to bounce along the eastern seaboard and then head back in the Atlantic."

"When the wind picked up, we knew we needed to pack it in," Geri added. "We lost the boat and all our supplies a few hours ago, and have been walking for what seems like hours. Finally, David saw this building, and we were hoping we could stay here until the storm passes."

"This is an old ranger station that I think they only use for a few months during the busy season," Theo told him. "The good news is, it has power, at least for now. You're welcome to share it with us, but we do need some help with a few things before everyone gets settled."

David tried to stand to help, and Geri did, too, but they were both weak from exertion.

"Tell you what…" Whitney said quickly. "You'd help us out more if you could keep your kids in here while we move a few things around in the other room. I'm a US Marshal, and we had an incident in here not too long ago. Part of that room is a crime scene, so we need everyone to stay away from it until we can get some help. We don't want to lose whatever evidence might be in there, but we also don't want to scare your kids. There's something in there that they really shouldn't see."

David and Geri both seemed surprised, but they obviously didn't feel threatened by Theo or Whitney because they nodded and sat back against the wall, cradling their children. Whitney handed Melissa over to her mother, and although the girl protested a bit, she went willingly.

"We'll be back soon. Please just wait in here for a few minutes," Theo added. They waved at the family, then closed the door behind them as they went to do something about Shorty's body.

"We can't move it," Whitney whispered, hoping that if she kept her voice low enough, she wouldn't scare the children. "That would destroy the crime scene. But we can hide it." She motioned to two of the desks. "Let's turn these on their sides and block off the area so they can't get around the counter."

"Good idea," he agreed.

They cleared off everything from two of the desks and stacked the papers and other items neatly on the floor in the storage room. Then they lifted the first desk and moved it to where they wanted it, then flipped it over on its side. The second desk was a bit heavier, but they did the same, and managed to do a good job of concealing the body without touching it.

"Hang on a second," Theo told her. "I've got an idea of my own." He went into the storage closet and returned a few minutes later with four of the park shirts he'd found when they had been searching the storage room when they had been locked in. "Can we cover him up with these, just in case the kids happen to get too close to the desks?"

"Good thinking," Whitney agreed. While he took care of that part of the project, she found a roll of masking tape in the storage room, and put a strip of tape on the floor from one wall to the other.

Theo finished covering the body then joined Whitney. "What are you doing?"

She finished the job and stood. "I figured we tell them that nobody is allowed to cross this line. That way, there will be a lot less chance of anyone being traumatized by seeing the blood or the body."

"We still might have to explain to David and Geri what's going on, even though we don't want to bring them into the middle of our problems."

"Agreed," she answered, "but I don't want to discuss it in front of the kids. We'll have to wait for the right moment."

Theo lightly touched her shoulder. "Are you doing okay? You seemed pretty upset about the family's arrival."

She looked up and met his eyes. "Is that your second question?" she said with a sigh, referring back to their earlier game.

He smiled, but it was a sweet smile, filled with reassurance. "Only if you want to talk about it. I don't want to pressure you."

She took a deep breath. Theo had managed to tell her about the deaths of his wife and daughter, even though she knew it had been extremely difficult for him. Could she share the doctor's news? She looked deep into his sapphire-blue eyes and knew instinctively that she could trust him. "I got some bad news right before I came to the Keys on my vacation. In fact, the news is why I left Tallahassee in the first place. I just needed to get away." She choked on a sob, but took a moment to pull herself together.

Theo placed his hand on her back and rubbed it gently, giving her encouragement just by his simple touch. He said nothing, just waited patiently for her to continue whenever she was ready.

She took another deep breath and swallowed hard. "I've always wanted to get married some day and have a family," she said softly, "but I was bleeding a lot, and no one seemed to know why. Then I went to a specialist and she found that I have uterine fibroids."

"Ah," Theo intoned. "I'm so sorry. Were you in a lot of pain?"

Whitney closed her eyes for a moment and gathered her strength. "No, they are annoying, but not painful. They did a lot of tests, and found the tumors both inside and outside my uterus. Because of where they are located and the size of the tumors, they didn't want to remove them surgically. As a result, I'm now infertile. I'll never be able to have a baby."

"That must have been devastating news to hear. Did your doctor explain that those tumors aren't life-threatening to you? If not, you should know that they almost never grow into cancerous tumors. That's a good thing."

"That's the only good thing about them," Whitney said bitterly. "Apparently they can be caused by genetics, so the doctors think most likely I inherited the genes from my family."

"That's true," Theo agreed. "But sometimes women can get pregnant even with the fibroids. Have you gotten a second opinion?"

"Not yet," Whitney stated flatly. "I was so devastated by the test results that I just had to have a change in scenery." She wrapped her arms around her waist. "I'm not sure it would do any good anyway. According to my doctor, some women can get pregnant anyway, but I probably can't because of where they are located and their size."

"You need a second opinion," Theo reiterated. "But even if the results are confirmed, you can still lead a long and healthy life with the fibroids. They won't shorten your life span. If they start causing you pain, you can usually have at least some of them surgically removed so you can be more comfortable."

"I don't care about that," Whitney said as she wiped her eyes. She hadn't wanted to cry in front of him, but she hadn't been able to stop it once the tears had come. "I just really wanted to be a mom, and now I know I never will be. The news overwhelmed me, and made me question my entire existence."

"There are other ways to be a mom," Theo murmured. He suddenly moved closer and wrapped his arms around her, giving her the support and strength she suddenly needed so desperately. She leaned into his embrace. "You can adopt, or be a foster parent."

"Yes, I can do those things—" she sniffled "—but no one will ever want to marry me if I can't have children."

"What?" He looked her in the eye, clearly surprised by her words.

"I was dating a man for the last two years. He had asked me to marry him. When I started having pain, he was supportive, up until we discovered the cause." She released a quavering breath. "The day I got the doctor's diagnosis, he packed up and left Tallahassee. He said a clean break was best and that he'd been considering a job over in Alabama for a while anyway, so now was a good time to call it quits. I haven't heard from him since."

Theo tightened his embrace. "You're better off."

"Probably," Whitney agreed. "But that doesn't make it hurt any less."

Theo was shocked at Whitney's former fiancé's behavior. What kind of man would bail on her for a medical condition she had no control over? It was appalling. Having a child had been amazing. He had loved his daughter with every fiber of his being. Yet, if his wife had been unable to conceive, they would still have been happy together. He'd never really understood some people's attitudes toward adoption, but there were definitely a few that believed they couldn't love a child unless it was blood-related and resembled them in some shape or fashion. Still, who was he to judge? He had his own host of problems. The bottom line here was Whitney and her feelings of self-worth that had obviously been trampled on by her heartless fiancé.

"Whitney, I do know some people think that way, but certainly not all of us subscribe to that belief. Whether or not you get healed from these tumors, you can still find love and have a meaningful, long-lasting relationship with a husband. You know that verse in Psalms, right? 'Delight thyself also in the Lord, and He shall give thee the desires of thine heart.' Your desires might change a bit, but God is a big God. Nothing can stop an unstoppable God like ours." He smiled. "Hey, isn't that a song by Sanctus Real?"

"You really think so?" she asked, still fighting to keep the tears at bay.

"I know so," he said firmly. "God has a plan for you. It may not look like what you expected, but that doesn't mean it isn't wonderful."

She sniffed. "Do you believe the same thing for yourself?"

Ah, there was the problem. He did believe everything he had just told Whitney. God could do anything, including heal her tumors, or help her find a meaningful life down another path. Maybe He would choose to make her a mother through adoption. Or perhaps she could find satisfaction another way. There were dozens of possibilities available to her. And there were plenty of men in the world who would be eager to be by her side while she went down any of those roads. Nothing was too hard for God.

Whitney was an amazing woman. Not only was she beautiful on the outside, she was also beautiful on the inside. Now that her loser fiancé was out of the picture, Theo was sure someone would come along and be delighted to share Whitney's life with her.

His case, however, was much less certain. Whitney had done nothing to cause her medical condition. She was completely innocent.

He was not.

"I don't know," he hedged. "My situation is very different."

"Different how?"

He sighed. This part of his story he hadn't shared with any other person on the planet. Yet with everything he'd been through during the last couple of days, he actually felt safe sharing it with Whitney.

"I told you I was on duty when my wife and daughter were brought into the emergency room. Usually doctors aren't allowed to work on family, but I had no choice because we had so many accident victims show up at the same time. That's not supposed to happen either, but it was a perfect storm and nobody else was available. Anyway, I hesitated when I saw them. I didn't move fast enough. If I had just done a better job, they might have survived…"

Whitney turned and looked him in the eye. The sad, disheartened woman who had stood before him just moments before had suddenly transformed into a forceful, defensive warrior. What really gave him pause, however, was that she was ready to defend *him*. "Says who? Was there an inquiry after the accident?"

Theo shook his head. "No, nothing like that."

"Well, did another doctor say or do something to make you think you made a mistake or should have acted differently?" Her voice had an edge.

He shook his head again. "No."

Whitney put her hands on her hips. "So you're telling me that if you had met them at the emergency room door when they were being unloaded from the ambulance, there would have been a different outcome?"

Theo said nothing and she pressed on. "Or if a different doctor had helped them, they would have survived?"

He still didn't answer her, but looked away, unable to meet her eyes. She wouldn't let him off the hook though, and moved so he had no choice but to lock eyes with her again.

"Then tell me exactly what you would have done differently that would have changed things."

Theo took a step back. He didn't want to talk about this, after all. He had analyzed and torn apart that day and every one of his actions over and over again in his mind. It was like pulling the scab off a bloody wound that just wouldn't heal. "I don't want to discuss it."

"I see that, but something tells me you *need* to talk about this." Whitney took a step forward. "Would a different procedure have changed the outcome?"

"No."

"A different medicine?"

"No."

Her voice softened. "Then I don't understand."

"There was nothing definitive. I just know if I were a better doctor, they wouldn't have died."

Whitney was silent for several moments and just stood there, looking at him. He didn't see pity in her eyes, or condemnation. He wasn't sure what it was. When she finally did speak, he found that he was anxious to hear her opinion, despite his reticence in even discussing the subject.

"Bad things happen to good people, Theo. The Bible doesn't say that if you're a Christian, your life will be carefree. You went through a tragedy, a *horrible* one, but God hasn't left you. And, He still has a plan for you, just like you say He has for me."

She reached over and squeezed his hand. "You need to forgive yourself. Sometimes, people die and there just isn't anything you or anyone else can do to stop it. You weren't to blame for their deaths. I wasn't there, but from what I know of you, I am absolutely positive that you did everything imaginable you could to save them."

Theo drew his lips into a thin line. Her kindness was his undoing, and he felt tears in his eyes. "It's easier to blame myself than to believe that."

"I'm sure it is. But sometimes life just isn't fair. Things happen that are out of our control. And yet, God is still with us, during the good times and during the bad. Maybe both of us just really need to remember that."

He wiped the tears from his eyes. "It's just so hard."

"Yes. I know." She took a step closer. "Believe me, I know."

Theo pulled her into his embrace and just held her, letting her warmth and softness seep into his heart and ease his hurt and pain.

Whitney was the first person he had let break through his defenses since his wife and daughter's death, yet he wasn't sorry he had shared his doubts with her. It was as if a heavy burden had been lifted from his shoulders. She was strong yet vulnerable herself, and the mix was just the balm he needed to soothe his soul and put the broken pieces of his heart back together, one piece at a time. Perhaps his self-imposed isolation was not the answer. Maybe, just maybe, God had brought Whitney into his life for a reason.

FOURTEEN

Whitney shone the flashlight into the wilderness surrounding the ranger station. It had been almost two days since they had arrived by gunpoint with the drug dealers, and the storm had been fiercely raging the entire time, crushing everything in its path. Finally, the winds and rain had started to settle, and she had felt so cooped up inside the small building that she had taken to doing surveillance every few hours and making a couple of tours around the building, just to make sure they were safe and there were no criminals lurking in the mangroves.

She moved away from the building and headed slowly toward the water, making sure no boats were sneaking up on them or stored by the dock where they had landed. Swinging the flashlight around, she looked for any sign of movement beyond the wind that still blew lightly against her skin.

Fortunately, she found nothing.

She glanced up. It was around 3:00 a.m.—more or less. There would be no stargazing tonight. The sky was dark and the stars and moon were covered with clouds, making everything pitch-black around her. It wasn't raining now, but the air still felt heavy and thick. She could also smell the sea air, which was a mixture of salt and vegetation that made her nose tingle.

Then, suddenly, she heard a crackling noise and quickly pointed the flashlight toward the water in the direction of the sound. Several sets of glowing red eyes shone back at her. Her heart beat frantically against her chest. She took a step back, then another, slowly heading toward the building. The alligators were all in the water, but they were still way too close for her comfort. Knowing they were out there made her skin crawl, and the red reflective eyes looked eerie and creepy in the darkness.

"You okay?"

Whitney jumped and swung around, ready to fight. "Good grief! You startled me!"

Theo put his hands up as she pointed the flashlight in his direction. "Sorry about that."

Whitney relaxed her stance and aimed the flashlight away from him. "No worries. All those alligators just make me nervous. There sure are a lot of them out there."

"What about the crocodiles?"

"What?" She hoped she kept the incredulous tone out of her voice, but it was really hard not to show her dismay. "I thought crocodiles were an Austra-

lian thing. Are you seriously saying we have those out there in that swamp, as well?"

Theo shrugged, a smile tugging at the corner of his lips. "Yep, there aren't as many, but we have some. You can tell them apart by looking at their mouths. When an alligator has its mouth shut, you won't see any of its teeth. But when a crocodile has its mouth shut, its bottom teeth stick up over the top lip, showing off a toothy grin."

"Thanks for the tip," It was time to change the subject, and fast. She did not want to keep dwelling on the dangerous reptiles that were just a few yards away. "I don't know about you, but I'm getting a bit hungry."

Theo nodded. "That soup was gone on the first day, as well as everything we brought with us, and I'm getting a bit tired of fish."

Whitney smiled. "At least David knew how to catch fish, even in the storm. Without him, we would have all gotten really hungry." She motioned at the building. "Everybody okay inside?"

"Yes. Everyone's asleep." He gave her a playful smile. "Why aren't you?"

"I guess I keep wondering when the bad guys are going to show up. They've got to know we're somewhere in the park, and if Jose made it back to civilization, I'm sure he's reported where he left us. Since the storm is winding down, I imagine we'll have company anytime now."

"Are you really sure? I mean, if Jose returned to

the drug cartel, wouldn't they be interrogating Jose about the dead guy in there? For all we know, he got scared and left the cartel for greener pastures without reporting in, and hopefully, the cartel thinks we were killed in the storm."

Whitney shrugged. "Either way, we can't stay here forever, and our kayak is a mess. Have you looked at it?" She'd gone to inspect it on her first trip out of the ranger station, and had been devastated to see the damage the small boat had sustained during the storm. The hull was broken in two places, mutilated by blowing tree branches or other debris.

"No, but I wondered."

"I can't imagine that it's fixable," she told him. "And I don't know the area well enough to know if we can walk out or not."

"I don't think walking is an option. I think the only way to get to this ranger station is by boat or by helicopter."

"Helicopter?" Whitney queried.

"Yes. I would imagine the rangers will start looking for the Martinezes and any other family that might not have made it out of the park before the storm hit. Hopefully, they'll fly over and we can get their attention. It might help if we built a fire on the beach so they know we're here."

"Yeah, but then the bad guys will know where we are, too."

Theo exhaled roughly. "True, but that's a chance we have to take." He took a step forward and Whitney suddenly felt a tingling shoot up her arms. The air between them seemed crisp and electrified. "And yet, I'm not worried." His voice was soft, almost like a caress.

"You should be," she murmured, not sure how to react to his overture. "If you remember, they're the ones with all the guns. We're plumb out. Every time I get my hands on one, someone takes it away from me."

He took another step forward and Whitney was suddenly unable to think of anything to say. In fact, she felt frozen, unable to move. The flashlight was pointing behind him, giving off just enough light to see the glimmer of interest in his eyes. He reached up and gently trailed a hand down the side of her face in a soft caress. She sucked in a breath, surprised yet captivated by his touch. He leaned closer.

"Miss Whitney?" The tiny voice interrupted her thoughts and she turned abruptly to see Melissa standing at the door, her thumb wet from sucking. The little girl had obviously just woken up; her brown hair was mussed and her eyes were puffy from sleep.

Whitney let out a breath, unsure if she was relieved or disappointed at the interruption. She turned to Melissa. "What are you doing up? Aren't you supposed to be asleep?"

"I was sleeping, but I had a bad dream."

"Oh, I'm so sorry." Whitney leaned over and picked the girl up and held her close. "At least it's over now. Are you still scared?"

"Uh-huh," Melissa answered. "Mommy is still sleeping. Can you sit with me?"

"Sure, sweetheart." She turned to Theo. "Good night. I hope you can sleep a little before dawn breaks. I bet it's going to be a busy day."

"You, too," he said with a smile.

He said nothing more as Whitney took Melissa inside. Yet his behavior made Whitney pause. Had Theo really been about to kiss her, or had she imagined it?

How did she feel about it? A knot twisted in her stomach as she considered it. She liked Theo. She liked him a *lot*. Yet his isolated, loner lifestyle was one she could never adapt to, and she was convinced she would go crazy if she tried. Still, he was attractive on so many levels, and was a calming influence on her when chaos reigned. The best part about him, though, was that he listened to her and helped her be the best possible version of herself that she could be. He had definitely become a friend—a trusted friend. But could he be more?

Whitney sat in one of the office chairs, pulled Melissa into her lap and cuddled with the little girl. Once the storm passed and they all went their separate ways, she would miss this child, and the entire family, that had blessed her in so many ways. She had been touched by their selflessness. All three of the children had special needs, with varying degrees of issues. Melissa had Down syndrome, and the other two kids were on the autism spectrum. All three were adopted.

It was also obvious that the Martinez family was not wealthy, but had taken in these children from the state foster care system out of a sense of love and caring. Adoption was a wonderful thing. But was it for her? Whitney had never really considered it before, but when she saw the love exhibited between the Martinezes, she had started seeing it as a real possibility. She had never known anyone that had adopted before, but during the last two days, David and Geri Martinez had told them all sorts of stories that had encouraged and delighted her.

She snuggled closer to the little girl whose weight felt heavy and right in her arms. A wave of sadness swept over her as she dwelled on the thought that she would never have a child of her own. A child that she could cuddle with, like she was holding Melissa. But maybe adoption was the solution. Perhaps God was showing her that she didn't need her own biological child to feel complete.

Closing her eyes, thoughts of various possibilities began swimming around in her head as she considered what her future might hold. She sighed and hoped she could sleep for an hour or two before the sun rose and their quest for survival began all over again. But she found it hard to focus. She started to pray.

A few hours later Theo stood and stretched, his mind still spinning. The rain had come and gone again, and the air smelled earthy and fresh. Light was starting to spread across the sky, but although the sun had come up, gray clouds still covered the horizon. At least the wind had died down.

He stepped off the porch and saw a startled snake slither away to hide under the building. The creature made him smile. If Whitney had been out here with him, the reptile would have made her skin crawl.

Whitney.

What was he going to do about her? He had been so close to kissing her last night. If that little girl hadn't woken up and come out on the porch, he would have done so for sure. But was that the right thing to do? He was still struggling with past hurts and wasn't ready to open himself up to a relationship. And Whitney was dealing with her own baggage. Neither one of them seemed ready to start a new romance. But could he let her go? *Should* he? She was such a breath of fresh air to his secluded, routine lifestyle. And ever since she had entered his life, he felt alive for the first time in years.

But deep down he knew he wasn't being fair to her by leading her on. He needed to let her return to her life and he needed to return to his own without further encumbrances. Because the truth was… his heart had been wounded so badly that he wasn't sure he could make anybody happy again. Most especially a vibrant, effervescent woman like Whitney. He didn't have it in him. That's why he'd buried himself in the Florida Keys where no one would be forced to suffer his company.

Theo sighed. He needed to talk to her and explain before he ended up hurting them both.

The sound of helicopter blades slicing through the air broke into his train of thought and he moved farther away from the building and into the open yard area, scanning the vicinity for it. Theo saw it in the east and was pleased to see it was coming in his direction. He considered for a moment then waved his hands in the air, hoping they would see him. It could be the drug dealers, but he had to take a chance. The Martinezes and Whitney all needed a way out of here, and they were out of food and other necessities. He ran his tongue over his teeth. What he wouldn't give for a toothbrush!

Whitney suddenly emerged from the front door of the building, her eyes scanning the sky as she looked for the approaching helicopter. Seeing it coming toward them, she turned and said something to the Martinez family, ostensibly telling them to get ready in case the helicopter saw them and was able to land and take them to safety. Melissa came out onto the porch but Whitney shooed her back inside.

The sight of Whitney and the little girl made Theo's heart clench. He said a quick prayer, asking God to make the helicopter part of a rescue effort instead of the drug dealers arriving to kill them. If it was the cartel, they had no place to go and they would all be sitting ducks.

His prayer was answered.

As the aircraft approached, Theo could see the logo of the Miami-Dade Air Rescue Unit painted on the door and the underbelly. An emergency medical technician wearing a blue uniform, with a large red cross on his hat, was standing at the open doorway. He waved back at Theo, letting him know that they knew he was there.

Theo ran back up the porch, getting away from the open area so the helicopter could land.

A few minutes later the aircraft had landed, even though the blades were still turning. The EMT rescuer jumped off the deck and walked toward the building, ducking low to stay out of the way of the rotors.

He approached Theo and shook his hand. "Mike Kilpatrick, at your service. Did you folks get stranded here? This building is supposed to be empty." He turned slightly and noticed Whitney, who had just come out onto the porch to join them. He nodded when they made eye contact and shook her hand, as well. "Can we help? We're out here looking for people that might have gotten trapped in the park due to the storm. It changed directions so quickly that not everybody got the message they needed to get out of the park and take cover before it hit."

"We could definitely use a ride to a safe location," Theo said loudly above the engine noise. "This is Whitney Johnson," he added, pointing to her. Then he motioned to the area in general. "We sure are glad to see you!"

Whitney met the rescuer's eye. "I'm a US Marshal, Mr. Kilpatrick, and we have a situation here. There's a crime scene in the building that can't be disturbed. I also need to make a call into the US Marshals' office in Tallahassee. I can give you more details if you need them, but I'd rather discuss it after the Martinez family is safe and secure on your aircraft. They arrived after the crime was committed, and have nothing to do with it. They also have three young children with special needs that need attention."

Kilpatrick raised an eyebrow just as David came outside and introduced himself, as well. "That storm surprised us and our boat sank," he said. "We were lucky to make it this far."

"How many of you are there?" Kilpatrick asked as Geri and the three kids came out onto the porch.

"There are five of us, and Whitney and Theo, so seven in all," David answered, gesturing with his hands.

"Take the Martinez family first," Whitney stated in a matter-of-fact tone. "We can wait."

"Are you sure you don't need any sort of medical assistance?" Kilpatrick asked.

Theo shook his head. "We're doing fine, but the kids need food and shelter."

"We do need some sort of local law-enforcement officer to return with you, though," Whitney added.

"Someone official to help us process the crime scene."

"Understood," Kilpatrick stated, his hands on his hips and his voice grave. It was obvious he was curious, but to his credit, he didn't pursue the matter.

He nodded and informed the pilot about what he had found, then paused as he listened to the pilot's response in his earpiece. Once he finished the conversation, he turned back to the group on the porch. "We've been out for a while, and will have to refuel at the Opa Locka airport before we can return," he said, indicating the helicopter. "The problem is, none of the other first responders out searching are anywhere close to our location, so you'll just have to sit tight until we can return to pick you up."

He motioned to David. "Let's get your family on board and to the nearest hospital, and then we'll return for the two of you," he said, making eye contact with Whitney.

"There's an FWC officer at the hospital who will wait until we arrive," he told her. "We'll pick him up and bring him back with us. Apparently, he is the only one available right now to come investigate your crime scene. We've got several agencies out here doing search and rescue, and the storm left a real mess in its wake, so every possible officer in the local area is already pulling double duty helping out. Even the governor is down here. None of us expected the hurricane to hit land, and then it turned at the last minute and slammed us mighty hard."

"The inclement weather probably doesn't help," Whitney added, her expression grim. She glanced up at the sky where the sun was finally starting to peek out again from behind the clouds. It seemed like days since she'd felt the sun's heat on her face. Even with the sunburn, she'd missed it during the last few cloudy days. "I'd imagine that a lot of the rescuers can't even get out this far."

"You're right about that," Kilpatrick answered. "And we've gotten all sorts of reports about stranded tourists, hikers, and the like. We'll be busy for the foreseeable future." He motioned toward the helicopter. "For now, let's get the Martinezes to the hospital to have them checked out."

Theo nodded and both he and Whitney helped Kilpatrick lead the family over to the aircraft and get the family on board and buckled into the seat belts. They all said a quick goodbye to each other and Melissa reached out and gave Whitney a big hug once the family was secured. Then the little girl waved at her happily as Whitney and Theo backed away and took refuge on the porch so the helicopter could take off. The aircraft slowly rose into the air, then turned and started back in the same direction it had come, carrying the precious cargo back to civilization.

At least the Martinez family was safe. Theo looked over at Whitney, who brushed a tear out of her eye. She had changed shirts and was wearing a light blue Everglades Park shirt that they'd found in a box in the storage room. Yet even though it was fresher than her old shirt, it was still smudged with dirt. She had pulled her hair back in a ponytail with a rubber band, yet, as usual, much had escaped and was sticking out in several directions due to the wind caused by the rotor blades. Her cheeks were flushed, which he could tell now because the awful sunburn that she had sported ever since he had known her was finally starting to fade.

She had never looked lovelier.

How was he ever going to let her go?

FIFTEEN

True to his word, Michael Kilpatrick returned with the helicopter a few hours later, toting a tall, freckle-faced Fish and Wildlife Conservation Commission officer, as well. The crime scene took forever to process, but Kilpatrick had brought both Whitney and Theo a boxed lunch that some well-meaning group had been handing out to hurricane victims at the hospital. Thankfully, the box had also contained a complementary personal care kit with a toothbrush, toothpaste and sample-size deodorant.

Whitney wasn't shy about gobbling down her food, or about putting the toiletries to good use. She scrubbed most of the dirt away, then liberally spread over the worst of her peeling skin some lotion that she had found in the bottom of the box. The comb from the box had also been somewhat useful, but it had taken her quite a long time to tame her hair back into some semblance of normalcy.

Before even going to work in the building, the FWC officer had interviewed Whitney quite extensively, and he had taken six pages of notes about what had happened to her ever since she'd boarded that tour boat back in the Keys. Upon her insistence, he had called in her report and tried to contact the closest US Marshal unit, but after talking to the secretary, she'd hadn't been able to speak with anyone of any rank. The storm had really pulled all hands on deck. Every officer in South Florida seemed to be involved in some form of disaster relief as the area tried to recuperate from the hurricane. Many regions still had no food, water, or even electricity.

Theo approached her after the FWC officer had stored his laptop and gone into the building. His face reflected a mixture of relief and exhaustion, but Whitney noticed that he had shaved and combed his hair, as well. His box must have also contained a razor and shaving cream.

She looked into his eyes, which were creased and heavy. Had he slept at all last night? She was beginning to wonder. He had gone through so much, and all because of her. Whitney looked forward to the day when she could return him to his normal life and they no longer had criminals breathing down their necks. Or did she? The idea of saying goodbye was a dismal one, but yet one she knew was bound to occur. She couldn't avoid it forever. And she did want him to be happy. That much was true, even though she would miss his quiet strength, his sweet smile and his incredible eyes.

"Any news?" he asked.

"No. Unfortunately, not one local was available because everyone's out working the aftermath of the storm, but I left a message with the secretary. I finally was able to call home, though, and talked to Jake Riley, the leader of my team up in Tallahassee. I told him everything, and reinforcements are on the way, but it's going to take them several hours to get down here. If we can just avoid the cartel 'til then, we'll have a chance of surviving this mess."

"Our chances went up considerably when this helicopter arrived and there weren't any drug dealers inside. I'm still wondering what happened with Jose."

Whitney shrugged. "We may never know, but we can't let our guard down. We won't be completely safe until we figure out who El Jefe is and we arrest the guy. Any guesses?"

Theo rubbed his jaw thoughtfully. "It could be Captain Baker, but I'm thinking it has to be someone in government, someone higher up than a captain with the Coast Guard."

"What makes you say that?" Whitney asked, curious about his reasoning.

"I don't know Baker, but I don't think he would be able to get away with his crimes if someone above him wasn't looking the other way."

"You make a good point, but Baker could still be the man we're looking for. If he did have someone covering for him, who could it be? The Coast Guard is federal. Maybe his superior officer? Everyone has a boss somewhere." When Theo shrugged, she fisted her hands on her hips in frustration. "This is when I need my computer. If I could just do some research, I could really dig into Baker's background and see who he does business with, who his friends are, things like that. I bet we could answer a lot of our questions with just a few minutes on the web."

The FWC officer exited the building and approached them, nodding in the direction of the helicopter. "I'm done here. Are you ready to go?"

"Sure thing," Whitney answered. "Can you drop us off at the local Marshals' office?"

"I can get you to the nearest sheriff's office," the officer answered. "But after that, you're on your own unless they can help. Kilpatrick and I have been tasked with getting survivors out of the park. We don't want to delay any longer than we already have, in case there are others that are stuck and in a dire situation." He grimaced. "I'm sorry I can't be more helpful."

Whitney shook her head. "You saved our lives, Officer. We owe you our thanks."

The FWC officer offered her his hand and she shook it. "You're welcome." He appeared pleased but shy at the same time. Had she ever been that new on the job? He looked like he had just graduated from the academy last week.

"Did you know Senators Harvey and Pratt are here?" he said as he motioned to the pilot to start up the aircraft. "They came down from Washington to inspect the storm damage. I think they're going to officially ask the president to have this area deemed a disaster area so the victims can be eligible for federal funds to rebuild. We're going to fly them around later this afternoon."

Whitney saw the stars in his eyes and she smiled. "Are these the first dignitaries you've gotten to host?"

"Yes, ma'am. It will be quite an honor."

Theo got on the helicopter then turned and helped Whitney climb aboard as the rotors started to turn. The FWC officer and Kilpatrick followed her, and the four of them put on their seat belts and then their headsets so they could communicate and hear the pilot during the flight.

The rotor speed increased and the aircraft slowly lifted into the sky. They'd left the doors open on both sides of the helicopter, and a wave of hot, moist air hit them as they rose. Whitney watched as the building got smaller and smaller beneath them, then turned and saw the basket where Shorty's body lay, wrapped in a body bag. This helicopter and the first responders had been a godsend, and she felt herself relaxing for the first time in days. Perhaps they were going to survive this ordeal, after all. There had been moments when she had truly wondered...

A bullet suddenly slammed into the side of the helicopter. The aircraft dipped and bucked from the force of the shot, and Whitney grabbed Theo's hand and gritted her teeth. She glanced over at his rounded eyes and they both began looking for the source of the shots. Theo gripped her hand tightly, almost painfully, and his other hand suddenly rubbed his stomach. It was obvious that the sudden rough flight was bothering him, not to mention being shot at once again.

Whitney could just make out the shape of an airboat below them, but it quickly was lost from sight as the helicopter veered, trying to escape the onslaught.

Another bullet suddenly hit the tail rotor and then two more shots also hit in almost the identical spot in quick succession. Small bits of metal flew into the air as the blades broke into pieces. The fifth bullet hit the engine under the main rotor and Whitney could see smoke start to pour from the engine above them. The helicopter started to spin and Whitney gripped the seat for support. Out of the corner of her eye, she could see the pilot struggling for control of the aircraft.

"Hold on," the pilot yelled into his microphone. "We've got to autorotate to the ground, and it's going to be a rough landing!"

The engine had totally disengaged from the main rotor system and the blades were solely being driven by the upward flow of air through the main rotor on top of the aircraft. The engine's rotational speed had drastically fallen below the rotor rotational speed, so the pilot was desperately trying to fly the helicopter by using the freewheeling unit—a special clutch mechanism that had disengaged the engine from the main rotor and allowed the main rotor to rotate freely.

The tail rose and the nose dipped, and then the helicopter spun clockwise around and around as the pilot continued to struggle for control. The aircraft tipped to the right as it sank toward the earth. The top rotors smashed into the ground first, then broke into pieces and flew in all directions. Several pieces of the shattered rotor suddenly flew into the passenger compartment and lodged into the FWC officer's side and neck. He screamed in pain before his body silently slumped in the seat belt and a sea of red spread across his shirt. Kilpatrick, Whitney and Theo all reached over to help him, but their efforts were in vain as the helicopter crashed seconds later.

Theo turned his body the best he could to shield Whitney from the flying debris, but he was being jolted around so much by the crash that it was almost impossible to control his movements. He could see the terror in her eyes and was sure the fear was reflected in his own, as well. When would this nightmare end? The helicopter body bounced once then twice against the ground, the turning rotors breaking the fall a small amount as the remaining pieces embedded themselves into the wet marshy land. With a groan, the aircraft settled then sank another foot or so as water immediately started seeping in through the open door.

Theo moved his head slightly and saw the FWC

officer's sightless eyes staring back at him. Blood still seeped from his wounds, but it was obvious the man was dead. Theo turned his head, frantically scanning the inside of the helicopter. Torn and damaged machinery, broken glass and ripped fabric met his glance everywhere he looked, but his only concern was the other three lives on the helicopter.

Had Whitney survived?

He raised his head an inch or so and looked to his left, amazed that his rimless glasses, while cock-eyed, were still on his face. He lifted his right hand, adjusted them and then tried to sit up, forgetting for a moment that the seat belt still held him tightly against the seat. He reached down and unsnapped the belt, then sat up quickly and awkwardly pulled himself out of the straps. The helicopter was tilted at an angle, but he wedged himself against the seat and frame of the helicopter until he was free and able to move around.

Whitney suddenly groaned and moved a bit, and a wave of relief swept over Theo. She was alive, but for how long? He touched her shoulder, then cupped her cheek in his hand, needing to make sure she didn't have any life-threatening injuries. His heart beat erratically against his rib cage as fear enveloped him.

"Are you okay? Tell me what you're feeling."

She didn't answer right away, amplifying his distress.

Was he going to lose her? A knot of fear still pulsed painfully in his chest as he frantically checked her for injuries. Suddenly he was flooded with images of when he'd been in the emergency room working when his wife had been brought in on a stretcher, bloody and broken. He had checked her, too, and moments later she had died right in front of him. Would the same thing happen today with Whitney? A new and paralyzing wave of panic swept over Theo, freezing his muscles and making it hard for him to even breathe.

Whitney opened her eyes and took a moment to focus. He tried to give her an encouraging smile, despite the turmoil within him. He brushed the hair out of her eyes. "Are you okay?"

"I think so." She quickly looked around the inside of the helicopter, then returned her eyes to Theo. They were filled with worry. "How about you? Are you hurt? What about the others?"

"I'm good," he answered, and said a quick and silent prayer of thanks to God for saving Whitney's life. "The FWC officer is dead. Pieces of shrapnel from the rotor blade killed him before we even hit the ground. I don't know about the other two. It looks like Kilpatrick has been knocked unconscious, and I haven't heard or seen anything from the pilot yet." Theo watched her carefully as she slowly returned to herself and recovered from the crash. She tested out her arms and legs and relief washed over him. They had been thrown around quite a bit during the crash, but their seat belts had probably saved their lives by holding them fast against the seats.

"Everything seems to be working the way it should," she said with a touch of awe. "I can't believe we're still alive after being shot out of the sky!"

Theo smiled to himself. Even after a helicopter crash, Whitney was able to draw on her inner strength and wouldn't give up. There were no tears, just resolve and determination. She was one incredible woman. "Let me help you get out of that seat belt."

They worked together to free her of the straps, then turned their attention to Kilpatrick, who was groaning as he regained consciousness. The EMT's head was bleeding on the left side where something had apparently struck him during the crash, but it didn't seem like a life-threatening wound. Together, they helped him extricate himself from the straps and then turned their attention to the pilot, who was still silent at the front of the helicopter.

"Hey, buddy, are you okay over there?" Kilpatrick called. There was no answer, There was also no way to reach the pilot since the crash had virtually blocked off access to the cockpit.

"We'll have to try to get him from the outside," Whitney stated as she awkwardly tried to balance herself against the side of the helicopter. "I can't even reach him to see if he's alive or not."

The aircraft suddenly shifted and groaned as it moved in the marshy water, and the three of them gripped the frame to steady themselves. Dirty brown water was slowly seeping into the floor through the cracks and the holes the crash had caused.

"I guess we landed in the swamp," Kilpatrick quipped, but there was anxiety in his voice rather than mirth.

"Let's get out of here first and then see what we can do for the pilot," Whitney suggested.

"Hopefully the crash scared away the alligators and the crocodiles," Theo added. "But please keep an eye out, just in case. We don't want one to come after us because we inadvertently disturbed one of their nests."

Sudden engine noise assailed them. It was so loud, it was deafening. Whitney dove for the Glock 17 strapped to the waist of the dead FWC officer. She pulled the pistol from the holster, then chambered a round and slipped her finger on the trigger. She pointed the weapon at the roof of the helicopter for safety, her body tense but motionless as she assessed the danger.

Theo watched Whitney in silent admiration. Even barely recovered from a helicopter crash, she was ready to defend them all against this newest peril. He knew, like the rest of them, that whoever was out there in that boat was dangerous and an immediate threat. They had obviously been the ones that had shot down the helicopter, and had now apparently arrived to finish the job. Even with Whitney armed once again, he didn't see how they were going to survive even the next ten minutes. He felt like a sitting duck in a metal cage.

The engine noise increased then abruptly stopped,

but the drone of the propeller blades continued as the airboat powered down.

"Come on out of there!" someone ordered from outside the downed aircraft. The voice, heavily accented, was deep and menacing.

"People are hurt," Theo yelled back. "We could use some help." He met Whitney's eye and could tell that she instantly understood he was luring them in so she could fire at will to protect them, if needed. Theo smiled, despite the anxiety growing inside him, glad that they could communicate so well with just a look between them. There was a host of feelings and thoughts he hadn't even had time to process spinning throughout his head, but he had to focus on the here and now.

"Come out with your hands up. Then we'll help the others," the voice answered.

"We need help now," Theo repeated loudly. "We can't leave them."

The helicopter's angle limited their field of vision, so none of them could really see what was happening outside the cabin, but they heard noises, as if someone was approaching. The next thing they knew, a volley of shots was being fired into the cockpit. They all ducked instinctively at the sound, knowing that, no matter what the pilot's condition was before, he was now undoubtedly dead.

"The next group of bullets will go straight into the cabin," the accented voice said once the gun stopped firing. "Come out now or you're all dead."

Kilpatrick's eyes rounded. "Who are these guys?"

"Your worst nightmare," Theo answered. He turned to Whitney. "Once we're outside, I'll try to distract them. Then you take out as many as you can with your pistol."

"Hold on," Kilpatrick protested, putting his hands up. "They'll kill us all for sure if you do that."

"They're not here to save us," Whitney told him quietly. "They shot us out of the sky for a reason, and you saw what they just did to the pilot."

"Maybe we can persuade them…" Kilpatrick said, his tone hopeful.

"That's not how they operate," Theo answered. He turned to Kilpatrick and motioned to the seat where he had been strapped in only moments before. "Stay in the helicopter and don't make a sound. In fact, put your seat belt back on and pretend you're dead, just in case they look. It's the two of us they want. If they think you've already been killed, you might just survive."

Theo turned to Whitney, who was only a few inches away, and touched her cheek gently with the back of his hand. Their eyes locked and he gave her a small smile, knowing this might very well be the last chance he would ever have to talk to her and say what was in his heart. "I'm falling in love with you," he said softly for her ears alone. Then he turned, leaned over and started maneuvering out of the helicopter door.

SIXTEEN

Whitney was stunned by Theo's words, yet a wave of warmth and happiness spread over her, despite the seriousness of their situation. Theo Roberts, the smart, handsome, gentle-hearted scientist who had been her rock and comfort the last few days, was falling in love with her! Yet despite the love she had seen in his eyes as he'd spoken, the fear in her chest intensified. Was she going to lose him in a matter of minutes at the hands of the drug dealers? Whoever was waiting outside was obviously armed to the teeth and ready to kill them the moment they climbed out of the helicopter.

She hid the pistol in the waistband of her shorts and covered it with her T-shirt, then followed Theo out the side cabin door. Her feet landed in a sludge of muddy water and vegetation as she pulled herself through the opening, and she shielded her eyes from the sun as she made her way out, hoping there was no unfriendly wildlife anywhere nearby.

Three men waited outside with Theo. Two of

them sported automatic weapons that they pointed at Whitney as she emerged. The third, the apparent leader of the group, stood on the bow of the airboat. He wasn't holding a weapon, but she could see a pistol strapped to his waist. "Anyone else in there?" the leader asked as one of the two riflemen took a step toward her.

"There are a couple of bodies still inside, if that's what you mean," she said with derision, hopeful that her tone and attitude would keep them from checking and realizing that Kilpatrick was still alive and breathing. "Shooting a helicopter out of the sky tends to kill people."

Theo suddenly purposefully stumbled and shoved one of the men holding an automatic rifle. Bullets fired aimlessly at the sky as he tried to recover.

Whitney whipped the pistol from her waist and fired once at the man standing on the boat. The bullet caught him square in the chest and he fell forward into the marshy wetland, dead before his body even hit the ground. She quickly turned and fired at the other armed man standing silently to her right and fired again, just as he was bringing the rifle to bear on her. The bullet also hit center mass, and his body dropped to the ground only a few feet away.

"Freeze or that breath will be your last," a voice commanded as she felt the barrel of a gun press against the back of her head.

Whitney obeyed, instantly recognizing the voice. It was Kilpatrick. Her heart filled with dread as she realized she had made a classic mistake. She had assumed Kilpatrick was a good guy and hadn't bothered to check him for weapons. In fact, she hadn't even considered that he could be on the drug dealers' payroll. Now both she and Theo would pay the price for her mistake.

She slowly raised her hands. Kilpatrick pulled the pistol from her fingers and stashed it in his waistband, then lowered his gun until it was only pointing toward her chest instead of her head. "Go get in the boat. Now."

She glanced over at Theo, who was standing by the other surviving drug dealer whose automatic rifle was pointed straight at Theo's chest. The gunman motioned for him to follow Whitney to the boat, and the two of them slowly headed for the bow, struggling a bit as their feet got sucked into the muddy, spongy ground. A thick gray rope lay strung across the marsh a few feet in front of her, and Whitney did a double take as it moved. She screeched and stepped back several steps, pulling Theo with her right before he stepped on the rope. Only it was no rope. The water moccasin raised its head about four inches, his tongue slithering in and out as it cautiously watched them.

Gunfire erupted and the snake disintegrated into pieces right before their eyes. Whitney turned and looked at Kilpatrick, who was standing a few feet away, smoke still wafting from the barrel of his gun. It was interesting that he had killed the snake, but seemed to want to take Theo and her captive. Why didn't he just kill them outright? She wasn't anxious to die, but she did wonder about his motives. Did El Jefe still want to question them personally?

"Where are you taking us?" she asked cautiously, not sure what to make of him. She had misjudged him once and didn't want to do so a second time.

"You have a date with El Jefe," he said in a firm tone. "My orders are to make sure you don't keep him waiting."

"The man obviously doesn't care about you," Theo told him roughly. "He just ordered the others to shoot down the helicopter you were riding in. You could help us escape instead."

"I could," Kilpatrick said with a laugh, "but then my life would be truly worthless. He would hunt me down if I helped you, or even if I tried to leave the cartel. Nobody leaves. Nobody alive anyway. It's not something you can just walk away from."

"Remember, I'm a US Marshal," Whitney said fervently in a tone she hoped only Kilpatrick and Theo could hear. She hadn't forgotten about the other gunman who was about ten feet away, keeping a lookout. "We specialize in witness protection. You could testify and bring down the entire operation. Then you could start over again with a new name in a new location. I can make that happen. I work with a really good team of Marshals."

Kilpatrick paused as if considering her words, but

then a flicker passed across his eyes and his determination returned. "Get in the boat—now."

Whitney obeyed, but she wasn't ready to give up. She looked over at Theo and love swelled in her heart. They had survived so far. She refused to believe that their fate was sealed.

She watched as he got on the boat, then tingled at his touch when he turned and helped her on board. He was such a wonderful man, filled with compassion and quiet strength. Their lives seemed to be on totally different paths, yet against all odds, they had found something remarkable in one another. But even if they could never be together, she would keep fighting and doing everything she could to help him survive, no matter what happened to her along the way. She silently hoped that once El Jefe was behind bars, Theo would return to medicine and continue to use his gift to help others, even if the love he professed for her never came to fruition.

Once on the airboat, Kilpatrick pulled some zip ties out of his pocket, secured Theo's wrists together and then tied Whitney's. The guard kept his gun trained on them the entire time. Theo caught Whitney's eye over Kilpatrick's head as he worked and she winked at him, knowing that he understood there would definitely be another escape attempt, but for now they would bide their time. She prayed silently that they would actually have an opportunity to run. The chances seemed slimmer and slimmer with each passing moment.

Kilpatrick motioned for them to sit. Once they were settled, he took the seat directly behind them. "In case you get any ideas, I'll shoot first then ask questions." Whitney turned to see his pistol pointed at their backs and then noticed him taking out his phone to make a call. He said hello and listened to the response. "Yeah, I've got them, and am heading your way." He listened again, then hung up and stowed his phone.

"El Jefe can't wait to meet you."

"I'm looking forward to it myself," Whitney said lightly.

"You shouldn't be," Kilpatrick replied, his voice now resolute. "He wanted to kill you outright, but his lieutenants convinced him that you needed to be questioned first. He wants to know exactly what you know and how many others you've told about his operation."

"As if I'd volunteer that information," she replied.

"Volunteering has nothing to do with it," Kilpatrick stated firmly. "El Jefe has perfected the fine art of torture. You'll talk, all right, and so will your friend. By the end, you'll be begging them to kill you."

Whitney ignored his taunt, but kept her voice low so the gunman who had slung his rifle to his back and was now starting up the boat couldn't hear her. "There's still time for you to change sides. You won't last long in this organization. I've seen how El Jefe operates. If you make one mistake, you're dead. Help us escape, and I can help you start a whole new life in witness protection. You'll never have to worry about El Jefe ever again."

"It's too late for me," he said softly, and when they locked eyes, she could see that her words had tempted him. She wondered fleetingly what had made this man decide to join El Jefe in the first place. Kilpatrick seemed like a decent guy, but somewhere along the way, he had taken a wrong turn.

"It's never too late to do the right thing," she responded.

"Be quiet and turn around," he said roughly. He nodded to the other gunman, who turned the boat and pulled it away from the helicopter.

As the airboat skimmed across the wetlands, Whitney kept her eyes alert, watching everything around them. She saw several alligators, who were thankfully at a safe distance from the boat, as well as a variety of birds, and even two otters that were playing in the water. The thought hit her that if she was doing a boat tour, she would actually be enjoying herself, but the gun at her back made it clear that this was no pleasure cruise. She glanced over at Theo and her heart clenched. Was this their last day together? Would they both be dead in a matter of hours?

At least she had contacted her team back in Tallahassee when the FWC officer had let her use the phone. Jake and Dominic were certainly already on their way down to the Miami office. The question was…would they arrive in time to help? She took solace in the fact that even if they didn't arrive in time to find and save her and Theo, at least they knew why she had disappeared, and would continue the investigation into the heroin dealers, even after her death.

The boat continued its journey along the waterway, skimming over plants and marshland as needed on their route to civilization. Airboats could go where most other boats couldn't, so they were able to make good time across the Everglades since they weren't forced to stick solely to the canals. A fine mist of water sprayed over them as they traveled, and the land still had an earthy smell left over from the storm.

Whitney leaned back in her seat, her mind spinning as she planned their escape.

After an hour or so, the boat slowed and pulled into a U-shaped dock with a low roof. They were met by another man carrying an automatic rifle; he'd been pacing back and forth on the wooden planking.

The driver turned off the motor, jumped out and tied off the boat, then turned to help the passengers get out since their hands were tied.

Theo looked at Whitney, waiting for a signal of some sort. She was the expert—he was ready to follow her lead whenever she thought an escape was possible. He was fairly confident he could break out of the zip ties, now that she'd talked him through it and they'd actually done it back at the ranger station. But he was frustrated by the fact that every time they were able to arm themselves, the weapons were soon taken away from them. Whitney was good, but she couldn't stop a bullet with her bare hands.

He watched her now as her eyes assessed the situation. Despite everything, he didn't regret professing his love. He had learned his lesson well after his wife and daughter's death—he needed to express his feelings when he had the ability to do so. If he didn't, life could end abruptly and he might not get a second opportunity. He made a short, silent plea for help to God, and a prayer of thankfulness. They might not survive the day, but at least he'd had a chance to bare his soul to Whitney before death claimed either one of them. He'd never expected to find love again— had in fact hidden from it by isolating himself on a deserted island—yet love had found him anyway.

Slowly, Whitney had been weaving her way into his heart. She was so smart, so beautiful. And even though they had only known each other a short time, she *completed* him. That was all there was to it. Maybe he had been wrong to sequester himself after his wife's death. But right or wrong, he was done looking back and had resolved to start looking forward instead. God had brought Whitney into his life for a reason, and he didn't want to waste one more second without her.

The gunman on the dock kept his weapon aimed at Whitney and Theo as they got out of the boat and onto the dock. Kilpatrick followed, his gun also still pointed at the two of them from behind as they

followed the lead gunman as directed. Theo didn't
want to give up, but he didn't see how they would get
out of this one. Counting Kilpatrick, they now had
three armed men ready to kill them, and there were
undoubtedly more drug dealers inside the building.

Anxiety twisted in Theo's gut as the gunman led
them toward a small building that apparently served
as a meeting place for groups wanting to charter an
airboat ride. Designed for tourists, it had garish tropical designs on the walls and several picnic tables
outside with brightly colored umbrellas over each
one that helped protect prospective customers from
the Florida sun. He even detected a lingering odor
of fish and other fried food wafting over from the
cafeteria area. There wasn't a tourist in sight, however, but the parking lot did contain a sleek black
limousine and two black Chevy SUVs. Apparently,
El Jefe liked to travel in style.

A man in a Coast Guard uniform approached
them before they even made it into the building, and
Theo read the name embroidered across his pocket
as he stopped to address them. Baker was tall, equal
in height to Theo, but his hair was a salt-and-pepper
color instead of brown. There was a smug look of
confidence that covered his features and made him
seem unapproachable. His lips were thin, his chin
was weak, and his skin was red and mottled, as if
the man were an alcoholic.

Was this guy the mysterious El Jefe? He didn't
appear to be the mastermind behind a huge drug

cartel, yet looks could be deceiving. Theo looked him up and down, then frowned to himself when he noticed this man also had a pistol strapped to his side. Now they had four armed criminals, ready to kill them. The chance of escape seemed to dwindle even further.

"So, we finally get to meet the infamous Captain Baker face to face—" Theo said, although his words were cut off by a jab from the butt of a rifle right between his shoulder blades. Pain shot down his back, but he kept on his feet and was able to make it up the few stairs to the porch where the man was standing.

"You're a hard man to track down, Theo Roberts."

"Ah, so you know my name. I was wondering if you had a clue who you were chasing."

"More than a clue, Doctor. You left one of my men alive on your island when you went for your little boat ride. It wasn't too hard to put the clues together and figure out who was helping our Marshal friend." He waved toward the door that led inside the building. "Won't you join us?"

This time both Theo and Whitney got a push from behind, and the two stumbled through the doorway together. Whitney had gotten the brunt of the blows and ended up on her knees as a result. Theo reached for her, despite his tied hands, and helped her awkwardly back to her feet. They turned and faced the room to find three more men, all well dressed, sitting at a long table. The man in the middle was wearing a dark suit, despite the tropical heat. He also wore an expensive tie pin and cuff links that gleamed with diamonds.

Theo didn't recognize the man, but Whitney did.

"Well, if it isn't Senator Pratt." Her words got her a rifle butt from behind and Theo tried to bump the man with his body to protect her, all to no avail. For his trouble, Theo was rewarded with another jab from a different armed guard, but this hit caught his left shoulder blade and sent fire down his legs. He dropped to his knees but was quickly pulled up again by Kilpatrick and the other guard.

Theo met the senator's eyes, which were dark and malevolent. "El Jefe, I presume?"

SEVENTEEN

"Stop!" Whitney yelled as Theo received another hit for his words. This blow was to the side of his head, and bright red blood started to trickle down his neck as he fell to his knees. Whitney's heart clenched. She loved this man and simply couldn't bear to see him injured any further. Leaning toward Theo, she tried to block the aggressor. But the guard behind her pulled her away and held her arms tightly, keeping her a few feet away from the fray. She pulled at his grip, but was unable to break free. Then the guard yanked Theo to his feet, and took a step back once it looked like Theo would be able to stand upright on his own.

Senator Pratt didn't move, but the man on his left, who was wearing a gray suit, shifted on his chair. "If you haven't figured it out yet, you will speak only when spoken to." The man turned to Kilpatrick. "I understand that you let Ms. Johnson make a phone call to her office up in Tallahassee."

Kilpatrick's eyebrows shot up and his skin paled

beneath his tan. "I didn't have anything to do with it. The FWC officer on the scene arranged it…"

"You didn't prevent it," the man continued.

"It was out of my hands," Kilpatrick said, his tone taking on a defensive but careful tone. "There was nothing I could do to stop it."

Senator Pratt frowned. "I find that hard to believe, and because of your carelessness, we now have even more Marshals investigating our operations. That is unacceptable. Your services are no longer required."

He nodded to Lopez, the man sitting on Pratt's right who Whitney remembered from that day on the boat when she had first seen him remove his hood. Lopez had cleaned himself up and was also wearing a suit, but he still stunk of cigar smoke and alcohol. The two made eye contact and Pratt's voice was commanding. "Find out how much they revealed, then take care of them all." He pushed back from the table and started to stand. Lopez stood next.

Whitney continued to pull against the guard's grip and he finally released her. She sent a silent look over to Theo then locked eyes with Kilpatrick and made a slight motion with her head. Faced with certain death, Kilpatrick had suddenly changed sides. It was clearly evident in his features. He gave a slight nod in response and suddenly everything seemed to start moving in slow motion.

She raised her hands and then brought them down roughly, breaking the zip tie. Out of the corner of her eye, she saw Theo do the same. Once she was free, she immediately reached for the gun that Kilpatrick had taken from her earlier and stowed in his waistband. He gave no resistance and she pulled it free and aimed it immediately at Lopez.

Senator Pratt might be the leader of the organization, but Lopez seemed to be in charge of the muscle and intimidation end of the business, so she felt he was the biggest threat in the room. Her finger released the safety on the trigger and she fired and hit Lopez square in the chest. He took two steps back and fell backward, dropping the gun he had already taken from his holster as he landed hard on the floor. Her second shot hit the man in the gray suit, who also toppled to his knees, then fell face-forward as the life left his eyes and his gun clattered harmlessly on the ground. She immediately aimed at Senator Pratt, but he was able to get out the door and escape outside before she could get off a clean shot.

Whitney instantly turned and assessed the other gunmen. Her third shot hit one of the armed guards, right as he was aiming at Theo. The henchman managed to get off a shot, but the bullet went wild as Theo ducked and crouched against the floor, unharmed. The man dropped his weapon and slowly sank to his knees, then he fell forward, blood seeping from a wound in his chest.

She heard gunfire behind her and turned just in time to see the second guard aiming at her. A gun went off again and she flinched but then suddenly realized she hadn't been hit. Instead, the guard that had been aiming at her took a step as a shot hit his shoulder. Then he fell back against the wall as Kilpatrick's second shot hit him in the chest. She took a deep breath as she realized that Kilpatrick had just saved her life. If he hadn't fired, the guard would have gotten her for sure. She nodded at him in thanks, then both of them aimed their weapons at the boat pilot who had dropped his pistol and put up his hands.

"Please don't shoot!" he yelled. "I'm unarmed. I don't want to die!"

"Watch him," Whitney order Kilpatrick, who already had his gun trained on the man. Kilpatrick nodded, and Whitney had little doubt that he would do as she'd asked. After hearing Senator Pratt order his death, she was sure Kilpatrick would now have no trouble deciding to enter the witness protection program and testify about all he knew. She hoped it was enough to bring down the drug cartel for good.

She glanced around the room and, seeing it empty of any remaining heroin dealers, hurried over to Theo, who had backed up against the wall in a sitting position. She squatted in front of him and gently touched his face near the wound on his head. "Are you okay?" Their eyes locked and she was glad to see the love and support shining back at her.

"I'm fine, but Baker and Pratt escaped. Baker went out the back door." He motioned with his right hand, then gingerly touched his skin near his head wound, testing it for pain. "What about you?"

"I'm good," she confirmed. "I'm going after them. Will you stay in here?"

"Yes. But please be careful, okay? Arresting those men is not worth your life."

She nodded at his words. "I love you," she said softly and then leaned over and gave him a quick kiss on the lips. "I'll be back."

Whitney suddenly heard the airboat that they'd come in on starting up. She ran down to the dock as fast as she could, while also seeking cover along the way so she wouldn't be a target to the two men that had escaped. Baker was at the helm of the watercraft; he had untied the boat from the dock and was just about to pull away.

She used one of the boathouse's support poles as protection and yelled over to Baker. "Federal Marshal! Drop your weapon and turn off that boat motor!"

Baker responded by turning and firing at Whitney. One shot went wild. The second hit the pole where she was hiding about a foot above her head. She waited a moment until Baker turned his attention back to the boat, then moved from behind the pole, aimed and fired two shots in quick succession. Both shots hit her target center mass. Baker fell back, dead, just as the boat was starting to pull away from the dock. The motor slowed then idled as the gas flow dwindled. The airboat floated innocuously into the nearby brush and stopped just a few feet away.

Only one man left. El Jefe. And, arguably, he was the most dangerous man of the bunch.

Where had Senator Pratt run to? She imagined he had gone to the limousine, but she had yet to hear a car engine, so she didn't think he had actually managed to drive away.

Whitney heard gunfire from the building and raced back up, trying to stay protected as she did so. She held her pistol high, pointed at the roof, as she leaped up the stairs and took cover by the wall.

After quickly glancing in the window, she pulled back again, safe behind the wall. The sight she had seen made her heart clench. Kilpatrick and the boat pilot were both down, presumably dead, and a dark pool of blood was soaking the floor beneath their bodies. Senator Pratt had returned and now had Theo in a headlock, his pistol pointed against the side of his forehead.

"Miss Johnson, why don't you come inside and join us?"

Whitney took a deep breath, then swung around the door, her weapon instantly pointed at Senator Pratt.

"I can see you're a good shot, but I doubt you'll risk it with this man as my shield." Pratt's voice was cold and filled with derision, like a man who was used to getting whatever he wanted, whenever he wanted it. "Now here's what's going to happen," he continued. "You're going to drop that weapon, and you're going to go to Lopez's body and hand me the car keys. Then you're going to let me drive away."

"In your dreams," Whitney responded. "You're going to prison."

"Not if you want this man to live," Pratt said tightly. "I'll shoot out the tires of the other vehicles. By the time you actually get somewhere to find help, I'll be down in Cuba, driving my '57 Chevy and living the high life."

"Shoot him," Theo urged. "I trust you, Whitney."

"Not advisable!" Pratt snarled, tightening his grip on Theo's neck and pushing the barrel of his gun even deeper into his skin. He took a step backward, then another, all the time dragging his hostage with him.

What if she hit Theo? Could she live with herself if she missed? A wave of terror washed over Whitney and her gun wavered slightly in her hand.

"Do it," Theo said again, this time louder. "Take the shot."

Suddenly, motion erupted. Theo elbowed Pratt in the chest and the senator loosened his grip enough in response for Theo to drop a few inches. That extra space was all Whitney needed to be confident of her shot. She fired once and the bullet hit Pratt in the middle of his forehead, causing him to stagger backward, lose his grip on Theo and drop his weapon. He was dead before his body hit the floor.

Whitney ran over to Theo and they embraced tightly, the fear and adrenaline pouring out of both of them and into each other. "I was so scared I'd miss," Whitney said breathlessly.

"I knew you could do it," Theo responded. "I trust you. You're an excellent shot."

"Yeah, but I've never had someone I love so close to the target, either."

He squeezed her tightly in response. "Thank you for saving my life. You're one remarkable woman."

"You're pretty amazing yourself," Whitney responded with a smile. She reached up on her toes and gave him a tentative kiss. He responded and kissed her back. It was a sweet kiss, filled with love and promise. When she finally pulled back, her eyes were filled with fire and happiness. "Now, Mr. Theo Roberts, how about we escape the Everglades and get back to the real world?"

He nodded and drew his fingers gently down her cheek. "Absolutely."

EIGHTEEN

Whitney turned away from the hotel desk clerk, finally checked out and ready to leave the Miami hotel where she had been staying the last six weeks while she had debriefed and worked with the local Marshals and various multi-county police agencies to shut down the drug cartel. The project had been huge, but once her team had arrived, they had all worked together to arrest as many of the drug dealers as possible and shut down the operation.

There had been many long hours and days that never seemed to end. But, ultimately, their efforts had paid off and her team had made such significant progress that it was time for them to turn the investigation over to the locals to tie up any remaining loose ends so they could return to Tallahassee.

She hadn't heard from Theo, and his lack of contact was breaking her heart. After Pratt's death, she and Theo had found the car keys to one of the SUVs and driven into the nearest town to report the events at the airboat rental building. At that point, Theo had been whisked away in one direction, while law-enforcement personnel had surrounded Whitney and taken statements and collected evidence, all with her input. They'd revisited the scene of the helicopter crash and recovered the bodies of those that had died that day.

Whitney had also made it her mission to check on the Martinez family, who was doing well and were now back home and entrenched once again in their daily routines. She'd also checked on John and Mark, the two scientists that had helped them when they'd first entered the Everglades. Both men had left the area right before the storm hit, and were already back in Gainesville, pouring over the data they had collected and writing their reports.

Michael Kilpatrick had also lived, despite his wounds, and had been a fountain of information about the drug operation. He hadn't had to enter witness protection, after all, since the threat against his life had dissipated, but he'd made a very sweet deal for leniency that Whitney had wholeheartedly endorsed.

Upon doing a bit of research, she had discovered that Kilpatrick had only started working as a courier for the cartel to earn enough money to pay for his mother's cancer treatments. He had gotten in over his head. But, down deep, he was a good man that had just made some mistakes, and he'd cooperated fully with the authorities before his deal was even officially in place.

She turned the key to the rental car over and over in her hand, knowing it was time to leave, but with her heart breaking. Theo had returned to his island a few days after Pratt had been killed. He'd been asked question after question until the authorities had finally exhausted him and then he'd disappeared into his life of obscurity. He hadn't even said goodbye, but had disappeared one morning when she had been out at the Coast Guard station, interviewing the guardsmen.

His absence had hurt more than she'd ever imagined it would. She hadn't been looking for love when she'd come to the Everglades, but love had found her, and now, she didn't want to leave it or Theo behind. He had saved her time and time again, and in more ways than one. Because of him and his encouragement, she now had hope. But what should she do? She had no way to contact Theo, and he apparently didn't want to see her. She'd had several sleepless nights as she'd muddled through her options, but she had eventually come to a sad, inevitable conclusion.

She had to let him go.

Because despite all that they had been through together, Theo was a loner. He wanted to be by himself on that island, running his experiments and writing his reports. There obviously wasn't a place in his heart for her, regardless of their feelings for each other. It was a bitter pill to swallow, but one she had finally come to accept.

"Leaving so soon?"

Hearing that voice again made her heart clench. A smile spread across her face and she turned, knowing who she would see before her eyes even settled on his face. Theo Roberts. Scientist. Doctor. The man who had won her heart and given her back her self-confidence and new hope for a future.

"You came back…" It was a statement yet also a question.

He took a step forward. "Yes. I tried to make it alone out there, because I wasn't sure I could put the past behind me, but now I know I can, and I know why God brought you to my island. My life was so empty before I met you. You've brought sunshine and happiness back to me, and now that I've found them again, I want to share my life with you. I love you, Whitney Johnson. I can't live there any longer knowing you're alive and well up in Tallahassee."

"Is that why you came back?"

Theo nodded. "Yes. I love you. You complete me."

Whitney breathed out and touched her chest in a nervous gesture. "What does that mean?"

Theo took another step toward her. It hadn't taken him long to realize he'd made a giant mistake by leaving Whitney in Miami. It had taken him some time to make the arrangements to close up the house and the lab, but he was now ready to make a commitment and move on to the next stage of his life. "It means I want to explore this relationship and really get to know you even better, if you're willing."

"Oh, I'm willing." Whitney smiled. "You've given me hope for a future, one that I never thought I could have. I can't wait to see where this new path takes us, and I don't think it matters, as long as we're together."

He loved her smile. It made her whole face glow.

Whitney reached for him and he embraced her tightly, convinced now more than ever that he was exactly where he needed to be.

She suddenly pulled back and softly touched the spot where his head wound had healed. "But how will this work? I have to go back to my team in Tallahassee, and you work in the Keys."

He leaned back so he could see her face better and he drew his left hand down along her cheek. "Well, while you've been working on the case, I've been researching options. If it's okay with you, I found a position at the Tallahassee Memorial Hospital Emergency Room. It seems they were short a physician. I start next week."

Whitney squeezed his hand. "You're going back to medicine?"

He nodded. "Yes. You've made me realize how much I missed it, and how wrong it was of me to just turn my back on that part of my life."

"I think that's wonderful, but what about all your work in the Keys?"

"I finished as much as I could and wrote detailed analyses of my findings. It's all ready for the next stage of the process, and John and Mark have suggested a few candidates to continue the work. I'll be helping the university transfer the project, which they've agreed to do as soon as they select the proper person for the job." He brushed some hair away from her face. "And I've been thinking a lot about your diagnosis. I have a friend I'd like to reach out to about your condition and get a second opinion."

Whitney nodded. "I've been thinking about that, too. I think that's a good idea. I would like to set up that appointment. But even if the second doctor says I can have my own children, I want to explore adoption. I've started researching it and there are a lot of kids, both nationally and internationally, that need a good home."

Theo's heart swelled. God hadn't replaced what he'd lost—he would never forget his wife and daughter that had died that tragic day—but God had never left him, either. And He had given him a new love and a new chapter of his life when He had brought Whitney to his island. God was good. All the time. Theo would never forget that lesson ever again.

He cupped her face in his hand and leaned toward her for a kiss, reveling in the softness of her lips against his own. He had found a fresh start with this remarkable woman and couldn't wait to see where God would take them next.

* * * * *

A detective discovers the hacker he's tracking is the woman he fell for years ago, but she insists she's being framed. Can he clear her name and save the family he never knew existed?

Read on for a sneak preview of
Christmas Witness Conspiracy *by Maggie K. Black, available October 2020 from Love Inspired Suspense.*

Thick snow squalls blew down the Toronto shoreline of Lake Ontario, turning the city's annual winter wonderland into a haze of sparkling lights. The cold hadn't done much to quell the tourists, though, Detective Liam Bearsmith thought as he methodically trailed his hooded target around the skating rink and through the crowd. Hopefully, the combination of the darkness, heavy flakes and general merriment would keep the jacket-clad criminal he was after from even realizing he was being followed.

The "Sparrow" was a hacker. Just a tiny fish in the criminal pond, but a newly reborn and highly dangerous cyberterrorist group had just placed a pretty hefty bounty on the Sparrow's capture in the hopes it would lead them to a master decipher key that could break any code. If Liam didn't bring in the Sparrow now, terrorists could turn that code breaker into a weapon and the Sparrow could be dead, or worse, by Christmas.

The lone figure hurried up a metal footbridge festooned in white lights. A gust of wind caught the hood of the Sparrow's jacket, tossing it back. Long dark hair flew loose around the Sparrow's slender shoulders.

Liam's world froze as déjà vu flooded his senses. His target was a woman.

What's more, Liam was sure he'd seen her somewhere before.

Liam's strategy had been to capture the Sparrow, question her and use the intel gleaned to locate the criminals he was chasing. His brain freezing at the mere sight of her hadn't exactly been part of the plan. The Sparrow reached up, grabbed her hood and yanked it back down again firmly, but not before Liam caught a glimpse of a delicate jaw that was determinedly set, and how thick flakes clung to her long lashes. For a moment Liam just stood there, his hand on the railing as his mind filled with the name and face of a young woman he'd known and loved a very long time ago.

Kelly Marshall.

Don't miss
Christmas Witness Conspiracy *by Maggie K. Black,*
available wherever Love Inspired Suspense books
and ebooks are sold.

LoveInspired.com

Get 4 FREE REWARDS!

We'll send you 2 FREE Books
<u>plus</u> 2 FREE Mystery Gifts.

Love Inspired Suspense books showcase how courage and optimism unite in stories of faith and love in the face of danger.

FREE
Value Over
$20